Faye lay on her side and watched Kent clean

To accomplish the ... become lovers. No ... was anxious to ge ... to be a relatively p...

Kent shifted. Faye touched her fingertips to her lips, remembering the way his mouth felt on hers. She wanted him. He, however, had made it clear he was not going to co-operate. What on earth could be wrong with him?

He looked physically all right, but then again, she hadn't seen all of him, had she? He'd made certain she turned away while he undressed earlier. If she just moved his blanket a bit, she could easily check out the situation.

There was a cold breeze on his leg. Kent grunted and rolled over, but the breeze persisted, dragging him away from the very suggestive dream he'd been enjoying about Faye. Kent opened one eye and saw Faye studying his body as if she was his personal physician, her expression one of confusion and relief.

He didn't know what the hell she was up to now and he didn't care. He rose and pulled her into his arms, smothering her exclamation under his lips. He was tired of being the good guy...

Dear Reader

You may remember that for Christmas 1993 we
brought you a special pack of three books placed
under the title **Dreamscape** because they offered that
something extra: an exciting touch of the
supernatural. If you enjoyed those books and the
occasional **Dreamscape** novel which has appeared
since, then you will be sure to love Alyssa Dean's
MAD ABOUT YOU. Faye is an innocent, lost in the
big city—and cynical Kent should know better than
to trust her...

Please do write and let me know your thoughts on the
books we are selecting for you in Temptation.

The Editor
Mills & Boon Temptation
Eton House
18-24 Paradise Road
Richmond
Surrey
TW9 1SR

MAD ABOUT YOU

BY

ALYSSA DEAN

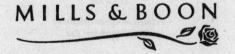

*MILLS & BOON and the Rose Device are trademarks of the publisher.
TEMPTATION is a trademark of Harlequin Enterprises Limited, used
under licence.
First published in Great Britain in 1995
by Harlequin Mills & Boon Limited, Eton House, 18-24 Paradise Road,
Richmond, Surrey TW9 1SR*

© Patsy McNish 1995

ISBN 0 263 79416 4

21 - 9509

*Printed in Great Britain by
BPC Paperbacks Ltd*

1

"WON'T LET YOU IN, eh?" asked an amused voice.

Faye whirled around to face a tall, loose-limbed man whose features were obscured by the darkness of the Denver evening. She took a step backward and he held up his hands, palms outward. "I saw you go in," he said, gesturing toward the sixteen-story building across the street. "The way you hot-footed it down the stairs, I figured the security guard had turned you away."

"H-he did," Faye stuttered. She clutched her purse to her chest and wrapped her arms around it. She wasn't used to the city. Its unfamiliarity frightened her. This stranger was no help, either. His brown leather jacket and worn blue jeans suggested he was a creature of the streets—something she'd heard about but had never actually seen before. She had no idea where he'd come from. When she'd stumbled, mortified, across the pavement, she'd been certain there was no one out here. At this time of night all the stores had drawn blinds and Closed signs on the doors, and the bus-stop bench was deserted. Even the neon Café sign was turned off.

"I was in the alley," the man announced, as if reading her thoughts. "Why do you want to go into the Rinholt building?"

"I—I want to see someone." Faye was more than terrified now. The stranger was at least six inches taller than her own five foot three, and there was something sinister about the way the shadows cut across his face, giving her only an impression of darkness. "What were you doing in the alley?"

"Shortcut." He sounded as if he found the situation amusing. "Did you call him?"

"C-call who?"

"The person you're supposed to meet. He—or she—can authorize your admittance."

"I know." Faye moistened her lips with the tip of her tongue. "The se-security guard explained that to me." She shivered, remembering the cold, uncaring voice of that particular gentleman.

"So why not call?" he persisted. "There's a pay phone right over there."

"I tried." Faye hugged her purse tighter. "He didn't answer."

"Had he signed in?"

"N-no. But the security guard said that if he'd been there since before five, they wouldn't have a record of it." She swallowed hard, blinking away the threat of tears. She hadn't anticipated an intercom system at the Rinholt building, preventing her from even getting close to the security guard. Now she'd have to try the back, go through the dark abyss of the alley. Her heart pounded frantically at the very idea, but she knew it was the only way. She took a step toward the street, forcing an over-the-shoulder smile. "Well...um... thanks for your concern."

He slid back into the shadows of the closed buildings. "You shouldn't be out here this late, you know. It's past ten. This isn't the most dangerous city in the world, but it isn't that safe for someone like you."

"I know." She wrapped her arms tighter around herself. "It...can't be helped."

"You could come back tomorrow. The building's open during the day."

"During the day," she repeated thoughtfully. She desperately wanted to grasp onto that idea, for a moment even considered doing it, but it was out of the question. She instructed her trembling legs to take another step toward the street.

"Good Lord," said the stranger in a completely different voice. "You're going to try to break in there, aren't you?"

"D-don't be ridiculous," Faye stammered. "I...um... Well, it's really none of your business, is it?"

"It might be." He sounded thoughtful. "For all you know, I could own that building."

Faye eyed his tired-looking clothes. "Do you?"

"No." She heard a smile. "I could be an undercover cop."

Her heart took a huge leap. "Are you?"

He chuckled. "Not exactly."

"Well then, um..."

"My name's MacIntyre," he announced. He stepped out of the shadows, revealing a long, narrow face, punctuated by the deep vee of a widow's peak. His hair, under the unreal luminescence of the streetlamp, appeared so black it swallowed the beams of light. His narrowed eyes were a similar color, wolflike, black irises flecked with lines of amber. The entire impression would have been sinister if it wasn't for the amused teasing in his eyes, the smile that hovered around his full lips, and the dimple in his chin. "Call me Kent."

He was now only a couple of feet away, smiling down at her with assessing admiration. Faye found herself returning that smile, as well as the admiration. There was something sensual in his languid movements, and in the way he was standing, his hips thrust slightly forward, his hands hanging loosely by his sides. "Kent MacIntyre," she repeated. Her voice was followed by a faint echo of his name: "Kent MacIntyre...MacIntyre...MacIntyre."

"That's right." His smile widened, he took a step closer, then seemed to catch himself. "Maybe you should go home. I'm sure your friend will understand."

Home? To her own safe little world? She'd left it only yesterday, but it felt like a lifetime ago. "No." She shook her head. "I can't do that. Home is far away."

"You're not from around here, then?"

"No."

"And you need your friend inside the building to take care of you?"

"Something like that," she said, nodding.

"Which floor is he on?"

"Um . . . I'm not sure. I think it's seven."

His voice took on a tone of suspicion. "What's this friend's name?"

"N-name?" She glanced over at the building, trying to remember the directory at the front. "Andrew. Arthur Andrew."

"The accountant?"

She nodded. "That's right."

"Okay." He looked up and down the street, stroking his chin with one hand. "I'll tell you what. You tell me your name, show me some identification, and promise to stick close to me. I'll take you up to Arthur's office. How's that?"

Faye studied him hopefully. Could this be the help her mother's people had promised? "Are you a Wizard?" she whispered.

Kent chuckled and shook his head. "No, babe, I'm not a Wizard."

Faye wasn't convinced. Hadn't her mother told her that Wizards were pretty conniving? "How can you get inside that building, then?"

He took a step closer, his exotic scent surrounding them both. "Without the use of magic. Now, what's your name?"

She hesitated a brief moment, then sighed regretfully. She should have known a Wizard wouldn't be this good-looking. He was just a kind stranger, that's all; perhaps one who could help her. "Anna. Anna...Ross."

"Anna, is it? Do you have any identification?"

"Oh, yes." She found the driver's license in her purse and handed it over, not bothering to mention that it wasn't hers.

He squinted at it under the streetlamp. "You're from Rapid City?"

"That's right."

"You sound like you're from Britain."

"Oh?" She'd forgotten about the accent. "I . . . was."

He handed back the license. "I'm surprised your name isn't Tinker Bell."

"Tinker Bell?"

"As in *Peter Pan*." His long-fingered hands gestured in a movement that encompassed her body. "If you remember, she was pretty tiny." His grin flashed again. "Although very well put-together, I understand."

Now Faye's heart was thudding for an entirely different reason. "I'm n-not that sh-short," she stuttered. "Can you really get into that building?"

"Sure." He put a hand around her elbow, his touch sliding through her thin green cotton blouse and up her arm, heating one half of her body. "Come along. Remember, stay with me, okay? I don't want to get into any trouble."

It's too late, Faye thought. She hesitated for a second, not sure she was capable of doing this. He raised an eyebrow, and she nodded. She had no choice.

Kent guided her across the street and spoke into the outside intercom with an air of authority. The security guard rose from behind his desk, strolled toward the wide glass doors and peered at the open wallet Kent pressed against the glass. The uniformed man pushed open the door, flicking a nod in their direction as they entered. "Sign in!"

Kent scribbled his name in a book on the desk, then offered the pen to Faye. Instead she pulled a pen from her purse and wrote "Anna Ross" in nice round letters. "Remember to sign out when you leave," the guard called as they started down the hall.

"You got it." Kent put his hand back on Faye's arm and led her to the elevators. "We're in," he whispered into her ear.

"How did you do that?" she whispered back. "What did you show him?"

"A security pass. I have one for this building." He motioned her to precede him onto the elevator. "Now, which floor did you say?"

She hesitated in front of the panel, then pressed a button. "Seven."

Kent rolled a shoulder against the wall, leaned his head back and studied her. His voice dropped to a suggestive drawl. "You really want to see Arthur?"

"I do," she replied. She stared at him, memorizing the dark angles of his face, the lean movements of his fingers against his rib cage.

"Isn't he rather old for you?"

Faye had no idea. "He's just a friend," she ventured.

"Good." Kent's lips drew up with wicked suggestiveness. "How long are you in town?"

"N-not that long."

"Well, if Arthur's too busy to show you around, I'll be delighted to fill in for him."

"Would you?" Faye lowered her lashes, resisting the urge to giggle. In this situation it was rather absurd to be flirting with a handsome stranger who, tomorrow morning, would be furious with her. "That's ... very kind of you."

His grin widened. "*Kind* probably isn't the right word."

Faye struggled against his charm and gave him a huge, grateful smile. "I really appreciate your help. How did you get a security pass for this building?"

"I work here, sometimes."

"Oh? Who for?"

"Stuart Investigations," he said.

Faye curled her fingers into fists, hoping her face wasn't revealing the horror she felt. "Investigations? Y-you don't look like a detective."

"Don't I?" He sighed dramatically. "And I try so hard. What does a detective look like?"

Faye could hardly breathe. "I'm not sure. I thought you were a street person or something."

"I know." He grinned. "That's what a detective is supposed to do. Blend in." The elevator jarred to a stop on the seventh floor. "Here we are."

Faye stepped out, with Kent a breath behind her. The doors whispered closed. Faye turned her head slowly, checking. The elevator was located in the middle of the building; to her right was a set of glass doors labeled Barkers Insurance, and to the left, matching doors marked Arthur Andrew, Accountant. There was nothing in the hallway, and apparently no one on the floor.

"There's no one here," Kent said into her ear. He crossed his arms over his chest; his eyes clouding into wariness. "How about telling me what you're really after?"

"I just want to . . . to . . ." Her heart slammed so hard against her chest that she thought she'd pass out. She put her right hand in her purse. When she pulled it out it was filled with fine, white powder. She glanced down at it, forcing herself to breathe. She had to do this. There was no other way. "I'm really sorry about this, Kent MacIntyre. You have no idea how sorry I am." She took one final look at his beautiful dark eyes, held out her palm and, ever so gently, blew into it. The white dust floated into the air. Kent stepped back, swiping it away with his hand, but it was too late. As the powder settled around him, he gave a shuddering moan, then crumpled to the floor.

Faye backed up, shaking with horror at what she'd just done. She scampered down the hall, searching until she found the ladies' room. When she located it she raced back, grabbed Kent's arms, and, although it took most of her strength, dragged him down the corridor and into the washroom. Then she knelt beside his unconscious body and struggled to turn him, which allowed her to retrieve his wallet out of his hip pocket. "I'm so sorry, Kent," she whispered into his ear. "Please forgive me." She pressed a finger against the faint stubble of his jaw, inhaling his scent, fighting the feeling that she'd done something she shouldn't have. Maybe she should have tried to explain, asked for his help. She picked up one of his hands, then dropped it, shivering. No, that wouldn't have been wise. She hugged herself, then pulled Kent's security badge out of his wallet. It was too late now to back out. Her self-imposed mission had begun.

"FOR PETE'S SAKE, can't you talk quieter?" Kent asked through his tensely bunched jaw. "That charming policeman treated me to the same lecture. Now my head really hurts."

Dan Stuart paced across his small, square office, stopping long enough to grace Kent with a look of furious annoyance. "Your head *should* hurt, damn it!"

"It's swell to see you, too," Kent muttered. He watched Dan's usually placid features tighten ominously and winced. There were few people whose opinion of him mattered to Kent, but this sixty-six-year-old man was at the top of the list. Now, because of that pixie woman, his standing with Dan had dropped a notch. He scowled at the thought, and the pounding in his head increased.

Dan took two huge strides to his desk, yanked open a drawer and pulled out a package of macadamia nuts. "What in hell did you think you were doing?" he snarled as he tossed the package into Kent's lap.

Kent unwrapped the package with slow, painful movements. "Helping a damsel in distress?"

"Maybe you should be a bit more choosy about your lady friends!"

"She's no friend of mine," Kent said bitterly. He nibbled on one nut, and then another. The pain in his head abated a millimeter. "Come on, Dan. It isn't as stupid as you and the police make out. She said she wanted to see someone in the building. I took her up to see him. I'm sure you've done the same sort of thing yourself."

"I may have," Dan allowed. "However, I make sure they follow regular security procedures, such as signing in!"

"She did sign in," Kent insisted. "I saw her do it. So did the guard!"

Dan's voice rose again. "The guard can't remember you coming in, let alone her! As a matter of fact, he doesn't appear to have much recollection of the night at all."

"The police told me that," Kent said glumly. "I get the impression they aren't taking my story very seriously."

"That's not surprising," Dan said, sighing. "Did you have to tell them you were attacked by Tinker Bell?"

"That's what she looked like!" Kent conjured up her image and resisted the urge to smile. "She's short, just over five feet, with silver blond hair, blue-gray eyes. A real cute little thing. She spoke with a slight accent— British, I think."

"You're right," Dan grunted. "You were attacked by Tinker Bell. She won, too." He tossed a laminated square across his desk. "She left this behind."

Kent picked up the square and stared at his own picture. "My security badge?"

"That's right. She used it to break into my offices. I've checked it for fingerprints, but it's been wiped clean."

"Wonderful," Kent said with a groan. "Just wonderful!"

"Oh, it's wonderful, all right. You can't imagine how wonderful it was to have the police call me at—" Dan pushed back the cuff of his striped shirt to reflect on the time "—six in the morning to tell me the security guard had found you, unconscious, in the seventh-floor ladies' room."

Kent shifted uncomfortably.

"What were you doing here last night, anyway?" Dan asked sharply. "I wasn't expecting you until this afternoon."

Kent sighed. "I got into town around ten, and stopped by to see if you were in. I parked my bike in the alley, and saw the woman. I felt sorry for her, Dan. She didn't seem to belong there, and she didn't seem to know what to do. She claimed to be a friend of Arthur's. I volunteered to take her up to his office. When she got off the elevator, she blew some kind of knockout dust at me and that's the last thing I knew until this morning."

"Next time, let me know where you are!" Dan slammed a fist down onto the desk. "My daughter-in-law phoned. She was worried about you."

Kent dropped his head into his palms. Dan's daughter-in-law was also Kent's sister, Avril. He and Avril had always been able to sense each other's emotions, no matter how great the distance between them. Although she was hundreds of miles away, Avril had picked up on the fact that he had a problem and, in her usual big-sister fashion, wanted to solve it for him.

"Great," he moaned. "The police think I'm crazy, you think I'm incompetent and my sister thinks I need a baby-sitter."

"I don't think you're incompetent," Dan said after a moment. "I think you're too easily fooled by a pretty face, that's all." His voice softened with concern. "You look awful pale, boy. Are you sure you don't want to see a doctor? I have no idea what kind of powder she used. I've never heard of anything that potent."

"Neither have I." Kent took a few breaths and straightened. "I'm okay. Really. It's just that same headache, and the nuts are helping."

Dan's lined face tightened into wrinkled concentration. "Why are the nuts helping? I thought you only got that headache when you—"

"I don't know," Kent interrupted. "I didn't do anything unusual. Go ahead. Tell me what she took."

"She didn't take anything." Dan absently rubbed a shoulder. "Amy's double-checking right now, but nothing seems to be missing. There's no indication that she touched the computer, but Amy will get on it as soon as she finishes going through the paper files. Someone was looking through them. The file cabinet was left slightly open. She must have used your badge to get into the room."

"She could have looked at anything," Kent muttered. "Are you working on something special?"

"Not particularly." Dan shrugged. "I'm looking into an insurance claim, and you already found that character who'd joined the motorcycle gang. By the way, his parents are suitably grateful."

Kent grunted a response. He didn't do the sporadic jobs for Dan because he wanted gratitude, or because he had any need of spare cash. Frankly, he was in it for a good time, and a little excitement. This case he'd just wrapped up had been particularly fun. He'd spent a week riding around on his motorcycle, wearing leather and acting tough while he searched various motorcycle gangs for the kid. As a matter of fact, this last week was the most fun he'd had all year, right up to the point where he'd met a sexy young pixie.

"I might have something," said a deep female voice. Kent carefully turned his head to watch Dan's right-hand woman, Amy Laxton, stride purposefully into the room. Amy was short, squat and middle-aged, and she ran Dan's office with seamless efficiency. "The McAllister file was out of order," she said. "It was in front of McAllaister, instead of behind it." She glared at Dan. "Did you touch my files?"

Dan quickly shook his head. No one, but no one, was that brave.

"Then someone pulled out the McAllister file, or the McAllaister file," Amy continued. "I checked the copier log. Someone made five copies between last night and this morning." She handed a file folder to Dan. "I think it's this one. The other doesn't contain five pieces of paper."

Dan flipped open the file folder as Amy marched out of the room. "Ron McAllister," he said. He did a quick check of the contents, and started swearing.

"Who's Ron McAllister?" Kent asked.

"He's a friend of mine." Dan shook his head, sighing. "Two weeks ago he was made acting head of security for Sharade."

"Sharade. The cosmetic company?"

"That's right. They've got a research facility on the outskirts of town. Ron doesn't know much about security. He was in personnel, but when the chief of security suddenly passed away, Ron took on the acting position."

"Why did he come to you?"

"First off, he wanted me to take the job instead of him. I refused, of course. He knew I would. I don't do that kind of boring junk. I told Ron to study the security plans, and probably leave well enough alone until they find someone with the right qualifications."

"That's it?"

Dan winced and shook his head. "Not quite. As sort of a learning exercise, he and I designed and installed a super-deluxe security system for his house. The plans are in this folder."

Kent rubbed his eyes while he tried to make sense of it. "This Anna Ross sure went to a lot of trouble to get the plans for his house. Does he own something valuable?"

"It's not what he owns. It's what he has there."

"What does he have there?"

"A copy of the security plans for the Sharade Research company building. I know they're there. I was going over them with him last week, just before he left town."

"This gets worse and worse," Kent moaned. "Don't tell me Ron's house is empty?"

"Afraid so. He's out of town this week." Dan shuddered, picked up the phone, and made a quick call. "No alarm was reported at Ron's house last night," he announced when he hung up. "Still, with the plans, it is possible to break in and not trigger the alarms. I bet this Anna Ross character is going to show up at the Sharade Research Lab real soon. Possibly tonight."

"I'll be there, too," Kent decided. "I'm looking forward to meeting little Miss Tinker Bell again. When I do, she'll wish she'd stayed in Never-Never Land!"

2

IT WASN'T A DARK AND stormy night, which surprised
Kent to no end. Considering the way this long, endless
Friday had gone, he'd been expecting pouring rain and
torrential winds. Instead, an almost-full moon had
risen just after sundown. Now, in the cloudless night
sky, it shone with determination, providing Kent with
enough light to watch the building at the bottom of the
hill.

The Sharade Research Division building was a four-
story, square building, ten miles south of Denver
proper, surrounded by well-manicured lawns, a duck
pond, luscious flower beds, and, beyond, acres of
wooded wilderness. It certainly didn't look like a
building about to be broken into by an industrial spy,
and the Sharade security people had assured him it was
impossible. Kent wasn't convinced, which was why he
was spending the evening up here, instead of comfort-
ably visiting with Dan and his wife.

He peered at his watch, then up at the sky, frowning
as clouds he hadn't noticed before floated toward the
moon. He should have guessed that today, his small
luck with the weather would run out. As the moon-
light faded, Kent heaved a huge sigh and held up the
binoculars, shivering in the coolness of the Denver

evening. It was inching toward eleven o'clock—he was tired, and very cranky. Wherever this pixie was, if she showed up here tonight there was a good chance he'd be less than cordial.

FAYE STOPPED IN THE main-floor stairwell, leaned against the wall, and listened. From the sound of things, the security guards were still unsure exactly what was going on. Not too surprising—about twenty minutes ago, she'd tossed a handful of iron filings into the control panel in the basement room; their security board must still be acting up! She'd found out what she wanted, and taken what she needed to take. Now, she just had to get out this fire exit and run the fifty yards to the safe haven of the forest surrounding the building.

She squeezed her trembling hands together, took a deep breath, and filled her right hand with white powder from her handwoven bag, just in case. Then she pressed on the fire-exit door, and slipped outside. The door closed with a muffled snap, she heard the hoot of an owl, and tried, too late, to change direction.

The shadows of the building changed shapes, forming and reforming in front of her, until they were shadows no longer, but a lean dark man who grabbed both her arms and grinned. "Gotcha, Tinker Bell!"

Faye stared up at the sinister features of Kent MacIntyre. She didn't scream. She opened her mouth to do it, but the last thing she needed was a lot of noise, and more witnesses. His fingers slid down past her elbows toward her wrists and she flung open her hand, tossing the dust into the air. It gusted into a swirl around him, and he hung on to her, but his grip loosened just enough for her to twist out of his hands. He waved at the air, coughing. She hesitated a moment, then whirled away.

She didn't have much of a head start, but it was enough to get her across the grass and into the underbrush of tangled forest before he could reach it. She ran as fast as she could, leaping over logs, crouching under branches. Her heart slammed against her chest, and her mind screamed with panic although there was no sound of pursuit, no suggestion that anyone was behind her. She kept running, until she ran out of the woods, and on to the dusty road behind the forest.

The green rental car was parked where she'd left it only ninety minutes ago. She ran up to the passenger side, gasping, searching for her keys in her bag. There was no sound. The road back here was seldom used. The noise of the opening car door seemed unnatural and loud. She slid inside, then pulled on the handle to close the door. It didn't close. Instead, it swung wide open.

"You might as well slide over, babe," suggested Kent MacIntyre. Faye fumbled through her bag, but it was too late. He was already inside the car, grabbing her wrists, shaking his head disapprovingly. She gaped at him in disbelief as he slammed the door shut and turned two dark eyes toward her. "Do you want to drive, or shall I?"

It would have been nice if she could have kept her composure, remained calm, perhaps matched his dry, lighthearted tone. She couldn't. She was too frightened to do anything more than sit perfectly still, both her wrists caught by the long, lean fingers of one of his hands, while he carefully lifted her bag over her head with the other. "I'm real anxious to see what you keep in this," he said as he laid it gently on the floor beside his feet. "However, we'll leave that until we reach the police, eh?"

Faye touched her tongue to her lips. "P-police?"

"Of course, the police. Where did you expect me to take you? Out dancing?" His voice softened to a purr. "Or did you think maybe I'd be kind enough to take you back to the Rinholt building, so you could confer with your friend Arthur?"

"I . . . I'm sorry about that," Faye said miserably. She hung her head, ordering herself not to cry. "I told you I was sorry." She remembered something. "My long-sleep powder worked on you then. Why didn't it work today?" He shrugged as she thought about it. "It was the same batch, wasn't it?" she wondered aloud. "Or did I get confused and put in the one with too much— No, I'm sure I didn't." She gave him a suspicious glance. "Are you sure you aren't a Wizard?"

He shook his head. "No, babe, I'm most certainly not."

Faye cringed down as that faint hope was dashed. "Please," she asked desperately. "Please won't you help me? I'm not finished yet." She gazed up into the coldness of his eyes. "I'm ever so sorry for what I did to you, really I am. Couldn't you let me go? Please?"

"Yeah, you're sorry, all right," he said sternly. "You're so sorry you'd do it again in a minute. Forget it, lady. You're one cute little thing, but I'm not going to be taken in a second time. You can deal with the authorities."

"You don't understand. You don't know how important—"

"I understand that you're quite capable of knocking me out again." He kept his gaze on her while he thought. "I'm not going to drive while you fumble through that bag, looking for another handful of knockout dust, and I'm sure not going to walk back through those woods again, dragging you behind me. There's nothing in here to use to tie you up. I guess you'll have to drive." He pushed Faye behind the steering wheel. "Go ahead. Do it."

"I—I can't." She shook her head, shuddering at the clenched set of his jaw.

"Sure, you can. Anyone who can break into a building the way you did can probably do anything. Come on, Tinker Bell, start the car!"

She kept shaking her head, certain there was no way she could. His expression showed his frustration, then suddenly cleared. "Drive to the research station!" he commanded, his voice softly dominating. It was an order she didn't want to obey, but did.

It took her three tries to get the key in the ignition. By the time she'd accomplished that small task, her entire body was trembling. She made an effort to turn on the engine, but there wasn't enough strength in her fingers to do it. She leaned back against the seat, gasped in some air and tried again.

Kent's hand on hers stopped her. "Don't be so scared," he said gently. "I'm sure being arrested is no fun, but they won't hurt you. Physically, I mean. There's even a good chance you'll get off—if you return whatever it is you stole. You did steal something, didn't you?"

"It's . . . it's not . . ." She closed her eyes, swallowing. "I didn't really steal something."

"You didn't? Why did you break in there, then?"

She struggled for an answer. "It was mine. I only took what was mine."

"And what was this thing that was . . . yours?"

"A formula," she said desperately. "A formula that can destroy the world."

He glared at her. "In a cosmetic research station? What'll it do, make all the women too beautiful to resist, so all the men shoot each other over them?"

"N-no," she stuttered. "It's a lot more serious than that."

"I find that a bit hard to believe."

She glanced at him from under her lashes. "It's the truth."

He heaved a huge sigh. "Fine. Don't tell me, then. The police will get it out of you, anyway. Start the car, and let's go."

Faye gave him a hopeless look, and turned the key in the ignition. She put a shaky hand on the steering wheel, and pulled out onto the road, while Kent kept an arm firmly around her shoulders. "Before we get there, I'd at least like to know your name," he said.

"I—I told you." Her heart was literally going to jump out of her chest. "Anna Ross."

His grip on her shoulder tightened to almost punishingly hard. "There are only three Anna Rosses in Rapid City. One is eighty-six, one is married with three teenage children, and one is a teenage child. Which one of these Anna Rosses are you?"

"N-none of them," she admitted.

"Good. That was the truth. Go on. Who are you?"

"Faye," she whispered.

"Faye?" He chuckled, shaking his head. "It's certainly appropriate. Faye what?"

She shook her head, feeling tears slip out of her eyes and down her cheeks. Underneath her jumpsuit, the two files she'd taken huddled against her skin. Her heartbeat seemed to smash into them as the road dissolved into a blurry haze.

"It's no big deal," he said. His hand stroked the back of her head soothingly. "The police will tell me anyway." He must have realized what he was doing; his hand moved back to grip her shoulder. As he shifted his weight, Faye's body moved slightly and something inside her jumpsuit moved, too. She jerked, stomping too hard on the accelerator.

"Drive careful, now," he warned. His breath seemed to give her courage. She bit down hard on her lip.

She'd forgotten about her necklace. She glanced around, checking their position. She still had time, if she was quick and careful. She swallowed, and made what she hoped was an innocent gesture to her throat.

"Do you know a lawyer?" he asked.

"A—a lawyer? No." She tugged at the cord around her neck, loosening her necklace.

"I do," he said, as if the words were dragged out of him. "I'll give you his name, if you like."

"Th-thanks," she stuttered. She felt so bad about what she was going to do to him. If there was any other way, she wouldn't do it. She slid her hand around the small vial on her necklace.

"I'm sure you'll be out on bail by tomorrow," he said.

Faye gave a strangled moan at his kind words, and ordered her hand back on the steering wheel. "I wish you'd help me," she said almost to herself. "It's so terribly important."

He sighed. "Lord knows why, but I wish I could help you, too. However, I can't. I have to take you to the authorities. You did two B&Es. That's a no-no, babe. A real big no-no."

Faye stomped hard on the accelerator and swerved the car to the left. His body jerked to the side. "None of that," he ordered as he sprang back toward her. Faye slammed on the brake, raised her hand and sprayed him right in the face.

The spray touched him as he landed on her. For a single instant she saw into his eyes, saw the expression change to realization. "I'm sorry," she choked out. "I had no choice. I'm sorry."

Ineffectually, he wiped his cheek where the spray had landed, his hand pausing in midair as he released a tormented sigh. Then his body went limp.

"IT'S ALL CIRCUMSTANTIAL," Dan assured Kent. "I don't think they have enough evidence to make a case against you, unless Sharade wants to get tough."

"That's not what the police told me," Kent growled. "They made it sound like the death penalty was looming in my future." He sprawled in Dan's office and looked around. "As soon as I opened my eyes, they hustled me down to the station, shoved me in a grubby room and grilled me for hours. For some reason, they seem to want to blame this break-in on me."

"You are a good suspect," Dan argued. "They found you, unconscious, on the road. It looked as if you had fallen while trying to get away, and had knocked yourself out on a rock. You had a file folder zipped inside your jacket that was labeled, Sharade Research—Confidential."

"Faye must have planted it on me," Kent grumped. "I told them she was there. They just didn't believe me."

"Since you're the only one who sees her, I can hardly blame them." Dan sighed and rubbed his eyes. "I don't think the Sharade people believe you, either. Apparently, they are pretty cranky about the whole thing."

"Yeah?" Kent put his hand over his mouth and yawned into it. "Who told you that?"

"Their vice president of research, Joseph Collings-wood."

Kent gave his head a sharp rap to wake it up. "Why were you talking to him?"

"He made an appointment." Dan glanced at his watch. "He'll be here soon."

"Oh, no," Kent lamented. He didn't feel up to dealing with accusations from the Sharade people. "What does he want?" he asked with some apprehension.

Dan leaned back in his desk chair and propped up his feet. "Guess he wants to talk to us."

"No kidding?" Kent's voice dripped with sarcasm. "And here I thought he might be dropping by for a game of chess."

Dan released a dry chuckle. "What's the problem, kid? You cranky because little Miss Tinker Bell got the best of you again?"

Kent dropped his eyebrows into a glare. "I also spent most of the night in the police station."

Dan didn't appear particularly sympathetic. "They held you for less than ten hours and didn't charge you with anything. I got the impression they couldn't wait to get rid of you."

"I don't think they like me."

"Of course, they don't like you. Detective Johnston told me you were a jinx."

Kent gave him a wide-eyed, innocent look. "Me?"

"Yes, you!" Dan's face was serious, but his eyes glimmered with amusement. "It seems that a file cabinet fell when Johnston walked passed it, missing him by inches. Two computers in the main office fell apart. Johnston's partner got some kind of bladder problem and was in the bathroom all night."

Kent snickered. Besides the mental closeness he shared with Avril, he had a few other unique talents that had often come in handy. One was the ability to slip a suggestion into someone's mind. The suggestion had to be something the subject would consider doing. Kent couldn't make somebody act like a chicken, but he could make them think they had to go to the bathroom, which is what he'd done to one of the policemen last night.

Now, he felt slightly ashamed of the chaos he'd created. "They weren't taking me seriously," he defended.

"You didn't take *them* seriously," Dan rebutted. "You recited a number of questionable jokes, and refused to tell them anything useful."

"I don't know anything useful!" Kent rotated a thumb up the back of his neck. Using his thought-planting ability sometimes gave him a headache. He pulled a package of macadamia nuts from his pocket and chewed on a couple until the pain started to subside.

Amy poked her head around the partially open office door. "Are you ready to see Mr. Collingswood?"

Dan nodded. A few moments later, Amy led a plump, medium-height, middle-aged man into the room.

Kent pushed himself to his feet and watched Dan greet Collingswood. The man was the embodiment of

an eccentric scientist, right down to his mussed-up hair
and rumpled blue suit. His pale green eyes blinked fre-
quently, as if he was confused by both his surroundings and the people in them. He certainly didn't look
like he was there to accuse Kent of anything, or to cause
any problems. As a matter of fact, he looked like he just
might be there for a chess game, after all.

As Collingswood turned to face him, Kent reversed
his opinion. Behind the confused facade, those pale
green eyes hinted at cunning, and a capability for cru-
elty lurked about the thin-lipped mouth. "Ah, Mr.
MacIntyre," Collingswood said smoothly. "I've been
anxious to meet you."

"Really?" Kent took Collingswood's hand and his
skin shuddered into gooseflesh. The room suddenly felt
warm and clammy, and far too small for its occupants.
For an enormously long second, Kent stared into Collingswood's eyes, both fascinated and revolted. Then
he broke the spell, and pulled his hand away.

Collingswood perched on the edge of a chair, and
fidgeted with his suit jacket. "Thank you for agreeing
to see me," he began. He blinked, looking around the
room, then over at Kent. "You don't think you need a
lawyer here, do you?"

"I hadn't planned on it." Kent slid his chair back a
millimeter. "Am I going to need one?"

"Oh, I . . . hope not. I didn't think you would, but I
don't really understand how these things work. We've
never had a break-in at Sharade before and I'm not certain how to handle the situation." He twisted his fin-

gers around each other. "My security people tell me that you were there yesterday, warning them about a possible attempt."

Dan picked up a pencil from his desk and turned it end over end. "That's right."

"They mentioned a young woman had broken into your office?"

"Uh-huh."

Collingswood turned to Kent. "The police said you saw this young woman again last night. Is that correct?"

Kent raised a shoulder and nodded.

"The police showed me a composite sketch you put together yesterday. Is that the woman?"

Kent nodded again.

"Did she tell you her name?"

Kent hesitated. He didn't feel like telling this man anything, but he couldn't think of a good reason not to do so. Besides, he'd told it all to the police. "She said her name was Faye," he admitted. "She didn't give me the rest of it."

"Did she say what she was doing there?"

Again, Kent hesitated. "She said she was trying to save the world."

"Save the world?" Collingswood repeated. "Good heavens. That's a new justification for industrial espionage."

"Industrial espionage?" Dan glanced over at Kent, then back to Collingswood. "That's what this was?"

"Yes." Collingswood shifted his weight in the chair. "I really don't want this to get out, but I think she was after our new acne-cream formula. I don't have any proof of that, and nothing appears to have been taken—except the budget projection files they found with Mr. MacIntyre."

"Acne cream?" Kent sat up straighter. "You mean she went through all that for a . . . pimple?"

Collingswood looked at Dan. "That's what I've told the police."

"Ah," said Dan. "I see."

Collingswood faced Kent. "I know the police took you in last night, but I just don't think— I mean, you gentlemen aren't in the industrial espionage business. If you're telling the truth about the woman, it could be that . . ." He sighed and messed his hair again.

"I'm telling the truth." Kent took a peek at Dan. The older man was leaning back in his chair, running the tip of his pencil across his chin, but there was nothing in his face to give away his thoughts.

Collingswood went on. "The police seem pretty convinced you're the one responsible. I spoke with my head office this morning, and they are prepared to proceed."

"Proceed?" Kent echoed. "With what?"

"Prosecuting you. They intend to make an example of you, Mr. MacIntyre. That's how they put it to me."

"There's not a whole lot of evidence against my associate," Dan said gently. "I don't think—"

"Sharade is a very large company," Collingswood interrupted. "They have a lot of resources at their disposal." He held up a hand. "Don't get me wrong. I believe you are completely innocent. However, with no proof, and without the woman, it's difficult to convince anyone else. I don't even think the police believe it."

"Me neither," Kent agreed.

Collingswood folded his hands primly in his lap. "I assume you're going to try to find her?"

"I don't know," said Dan. "It is a police investigation, and they don't appreciate—"

"Come, come," cooed Collingswood. "You are a detective agency, aren't you? It's only logical to assume that you would want to find the woman who framed you."

The front legs of Dan's chair landed gently on the floor. "What's your point, Mr. Collingswood?"

"It seems to me that we have a mutual problem, here. You, Mr. Stuart, must want this woman found. It was because of your files that she was able to break into our labs. And your associate here . . ." He pointed a thumb in Kent's direction. "Well, he's got to want to find her. Otherwise, he'll be charged. Isn't that true?"

Kent opened his mouth, Dan raised a warning finger, and Kent subsided.

Collingswood looked from one to the other, then continued. "As for me, I want her found, as well. If she took that formula, then I want to know who she sold it to. If she was after something else, I need to know what, and why."

Dan chewed on the edge of the pencil. "That may be true, but . . ."

"I've asked head office for a little time, to allow me to arrange for an investigation to be conducted." Collingswood peered myopically at Dan and Kent. "If that's not going to happen, well, I will simply have to tell them to proceed with prosecuting Mr. MacIntyre." He paused. "And your office, Mr. Stuart, for your part in this."

"Ah." Dan lifted a resigned shoulder. "I think I understand you, Mr. Collingswood."

"I thought you might. Now, I would like to retain you to find this woman. Not the Sharade company, but myself personally. Sharade is perfectly happy with the suspect they have."

"Ah," Dan grunted again. "Well, um . . . we don't have much to go on, and . . ."

For one brief instant, the expression on Collingswood's face changed from bewildered helplessness to absolute fury, then back again. "You are professionals. I'm sure you have methods at your disposal that I do not."

"Uh-huh." Dan put a hand to his forehead, sliding a finger along his eyebrows. "All right, Mr. Collingswood. We'll give it a try."

"Splendid." Collingswood rubbed his hands together. "Are there any papers I have to sign, or perhaps a cheque?"

"No." Dan's lips pressed together. "Under the circumstances, that's not appropriate. As you say, we have our own reasons for finding this woman."

Collingswood hesitated, seemingly embarrassed. "If you do find her, I would like to speak with her before we make any decision about an arrest. Sharade may well decide not to press charges, if doing so would not be in their best interests. You do understand that, don't you?"

"Oh, I understand, all right." Dan's drawl held an interesting note.

"Then you will let me know when you do find her?"

"We'll be in touch."

Kent was certain the room temperature lowered ten degrees as Dan and Joseph Collingswood stared at each other. Then Collingswood smiled, his top lip curling to show his teeth. "That's fine, then. Thank you, gentlemen. I'll be expecting to hear from you very soon." He shook hands with Dan before leaving the office.

Dan waited until the outer-office door closed, indicating Collingswood's departure. Then he lifted an eyebrow at Kent. "Well?"

"I'm a bit slow this afternoon," Kent explained. "Besides the fact that that Collingswood gives me the creeps, I'm not real clear on what he was saying."

"Allow me to translate." Dan perched on the edge of the desk. "Mr. Collingswood wants the woman found. She took something valuable from those labs, and he wants it back, real bad. It's not acne-cream formula, but he's not going to tell us what it is. He doesn't want

the police to know this, and he doesn't want us to snoop
into it, either. If we don't cooperate, charges *will* be laid
against us." He stared at the far wall. "Did I miss anything? Oh, yes. When the woman's found, we are *not*
to call the police. We are to hand her over to him. When
that happens, the charges against you will be dropped."

"Oh, my God!" Kent exclaimed. "Are you sure?"

"Positive."

"Damn!" Kent rubbed a hand along his forehead.
"I'm sorry, Dan. This is all my fault. I—"

"It's not your fault, Kent, it's that bloody woman."

"What are we going to do?"

Dan tapped his fingers together. "We don't have any
choice, my friend. We have to find that girl. If we don't,
you will be charged, and they will make it stick. Those
are the plain and simple facts."

"All right," said Kent. "Suppose we find her. What
do we do with her?"

Dan's eyes narrowed to navy blue slits. "I'd like to
wallop her but good for involving us in this mess."

"Who wouldn't?" Kent leaned back in the chair.
"Besides that, what? Do I turn her over to the police,
or Collingswood?"

"I don't know. How about if we find her first?"

"Okay," Kent agreed. "How do we go about doing
that?"

Dan pawed around the contents of his desk and
found a sheet of paper. "Here's what I've learned so far.
A woman named Anna Ross rented a car in Colorado

Springs a few days ago. The car was returned to the airport here at seven o'clock this morning."

"Any flights leaving around then?" Kent asked.

"Yep. Albuquerque, Phoenix, Salt Lake City and Las Vegas all left within a couple of hours."

"Great! That's no help at all. She could be anywhere by now."

"I know." Dan threw the paper back on his desk and picked up another one. "I've got a copy of that composite you made yesterday."

"You do?" Kent eyed him suspiciously. "I asked them for a copy and they pretty much told me to get lost. How did you get hold of it?"

"I'm a detective." Dan shrugged, using his usual line that meant, Don't ask. He handed a folded-up sheet of paper across to Kent.

Kent studied the fuzzy drawing. "It's not great, but it's close. Do you think you can find out anything with this?"

"I'll give it a try." Dan crossed to the window, closed the curtains and locked the office door. The room settled into semidarkness. Without a word, Kent put the artist's sketch on Dan's desk. Dan sat down, put his fingers on the picture, and closed his eyes.

Kent leaned back, waiting. He'd seen Dan do this a number of times, and it never failed to impress him. Dan could locate someone or something simply by touching a photograph of the subject. Kent wasn't sure if he could do the same thing with an artist's sketch.

"It's fuzzy," Dan announced after about five minutes of concentration. "Rocks, craters, no plants, no trees, no houses, no people."

"That doesn't sound like anyplace I've ever been." Kent dropped his head into his hands. "Actually, it sounds more like the moon. You're sure it's not a desert scene?"

"Pretty sure," Dan nodded. "It's too rocky. It's not mountains, either. There aren't any trees." He tried again. "Nope. That's all I get." He rose slowly to open the curtains.

"Tinker Bell doesn't live on the moon." Kent snapped his fingers. "Just a minute." He grabbed one of Dan's three atlases off the bookshelf and pawed eagerly through the pages. "Here we go. Salt Lake City, Utah."

Dan peered over Kent's shoulder at the U.S. map. "You might be on to something."

"'Craters of the Moon National Monument,'" Kent read. "I was there once. It's exactly as you described. Now might be a good time to check it out again."

"There's not much around there," Dan observed. He began reading names off the map. "Gannett, Carey, Arco, Butte City, Neverdale—"

"Neverdale!" Kent interrupted. "You've got to be kidding. There's a place called Neverdale?"

"Sure. It's in a valley near the Lost River Range."

"Neverdale." Kent rolled his eyes and stroked his jaw. "I think I'll try there first." He caught the teasing glint in Dan's eyes and frowned. "You got any better ideas?"

"Nope." Dan leaned back in his chair and propped his feet on the desk. "I suppose you want to go after her yourself."

"You bet I do."

Dan shook an admonishing finger. "Didn't the police tell you not to leave town?"

Kent wasn't concerned. "I've never been good at doing what I'm told. I'll go find Tinker Bell. If the police come looking for me, tell them you don't know where I went."

Dan scraped a palm across his jaw. "Oh, all right. You'll do what you like, no matter what I say. Do you need me to come along?"

Kent shook his head.

"In that case, I'm going to check into Captain Hook."

"Hook?" Kent repeated. "You mean Collingswood?"

"That's it." His face wrinkled into a mischievous grin. "You know who that makes you?"

"Peter Pan?" Kent guessed.

"Either that, or one of the Lost Boys."

3

KENT THREW DOWN HIS backpack and watched it vanish into the mist that was rising from the ground. "This is one weird forest," he muttered under his breath. He turned up the collar of his jacket, plunked himself down on the cold, damp ground and leaned his back against a handy tree. The stroll from the road to Faye's place was supposed to be two miles—an easy thirty-minute walk. He'd been wandering through these woods for three hours! Either the people of Neverdale had lied to him, or this forest was conspiring to get him lost.

Following the trail of the mysterious Faye had been a major pain. The people in Neverdale had denied knowing anyone of her description, until Kent convinced the hardware-store owner that he was a prospective suitor. After that, he'd been given a name— Faye Maxwell—and the information that she had lived alone since her father died. He'd also been provided with directions to her place.

It should have been easy: a ten-mile drive from Neverdale, followed by a two-mile hike north, along what was supposed to be a clearly marked path. The "clearly marked" path had been anything but clear or marked. His compass couldn't make up its mind about which direction was north. The supposedly small stream had been wide, deep and impassable but for the narrow footbridge he'd finally located. His mind kept telling him he was going in circles. A miserable drizzling rain had started, and then this creepy mist began rising from the ground.

Kent half closed his eyes for a moment, then took a peek through his lashes at the bushes. They moved slightly. A small brown rabbit hopped out and stared at him through wise silver eyes. "You late for something?" Kent asked.

The bunny considered it. Kent closed his eyes again. He wouldn't have been one bit surprised if the rabbit had pulled out a pocket watch.

The bushes rustled again. A breeze whisked past Kent's cheek and he looked up. A woman knelt in front of him, dressed in the same pale brown as the bunny, her silver-blue eyes wide and unblinking as she aimed an atomizer at his face. His pixie. Tinker Bell, herself. Faye.

FAYE HAD BEEN WATCHING Kent for the past hour, and wasn't sure if she should be relieved or terrified. Kent could well be the long-awaited Wizard, even though he had denied it. In both of their encounters, he'd ended up helping her, although his assistance had been given unwillingly. Or had it? "Be cautious around a Wizard," her mother had warned her. "They have their own special way of doing things." Perhaps Kent was on her side, acting in a typical, confusing Wizard fashion.

On the other hand, he could be working for the Alchemist. He did have a rather sinister-looking face, and he had been knocked out by her potions. Then again, the long-sleep powder had only worked on him once. Did that mean the Alchemist had an antidote for it, or did it mean Kent now had the special immunity of a Wizard?

It would be wonderful if he was the one. She already liked him, and she already thought he was terribly attractive. He was a slightly built man, not heavily muscled, but lean and light on his feet. She liked the way he traveled through her forest, choosing his steps with care, not crushing flowers, not stomping; acting like the visitor he was, instead of an invader.

She watched him for some time, uncertain how to proceed; too nervous to get close, too frightened to let him far out of her sight. Finally he sat down, leaned against a tree, and closed his eyes. Faye decided she was simply going to have to knock him out. He was much too close to her place, and there was too much at stake for her to take a chance on him. Maybe he was on her side—if so, he'd find some other way of contacting her.

She crept close, spray in hand, and knelt before him, forcing herself to do this. She didn't want to—she hated the idea of leaving him asleep out here in the cold dampness of early evening. It would be dark when he woke up, too dark for him to locate her place. He'd be forced to go back to wherever he came from. She might never see him again.

As she hesitated, his eyes popped open. The unexpectedness of it made her pause. He lunged forward, gripping her wrists, squeezing until the pressure of his fingers forced her to drop the atomizer. She stared down at it, then back up at him.

"Let's not do that again," he told her, his voice hinting at a smile. "Our dates are becoming so predictable."

Faye took a trembling breath. "Wh-what are you doing here?"

"Looking for you." Kent held her wrists firmly, while his gaze flitted up and down her body.

Faye shivered under his scrutiny, wishing she knew whose side he was on. "Wh-what do you want?"

"What do I want?" His voice rose slightly. "I want to take you back to Denver, and get me off the hook for breaking and entering, attempted burglary, and Lord knows what else." He took a breath and his tone softened. "I also want a few answers."

"A-answers?" Faye stuttered. It was damp out here, she was getting cold kneeling on the ground, and the pressure of his fingers was uncomfortably hard. Her physical discomforts were nothing compared to the agony in her mind as it raced in circles, searching for a way of escape. She didn't dare tell him anything—not while she didn't know whether or not he was the one.

"We won't talk about it out here," he decided. "We must be close to your place. We'll go there. You can change into something a bit more suitable for traveling." He tilted his head to one side, his slight smile showing his dimple. "I'm not going to molest you, if that's what you're so frightened about."

"It—it's not," she murmured. She hadn't even considered that possibility.

"Good." He transferred her wrists so they were held by one hand. "Don't try anything stupid, okay?"

She nodded mutely.

He pursed his lips, blowing out a sigh. "Okay, then, Tinker Bell, let's make tracks for Never-Never Land." As he went to stand up, his grip loosened. Faye gave a wrenching pull, freeing a hand. Before he could react, she snatched up the atomizer and sprayed it into his face.

He let out a yell when the vapor hit him, then he launched his entire body at her, catching her off guard, knocking her backward. He tore the atomizer from her grasp and straddled her, clenching her waist between his hard thighs and holding her hands above her head with one of his.

Although his actions startled her, she was too excited to be worried. She stared up at him, delighted. There was no reason for her potion not to work—he must have some magic of his own.

Kent didn't appear to be at all pleased. His entire face contorted, his eyes becoming thin cold slats of darkness, eyebrows huddled around them, and his mouth turned down at the corners. "You are never, *ever* going to pull that trick on me again!" he snarled.

"I won't." Faye smiled a huge, happy smile, not at all concerned about the precariousness of her position. He wouldn't hurt her; he was on her side.

"You sure as hell won't!" He glared at the atomizer, now resting among a pile of leaves beside his knee. It made an unusual popping sound, then collapsed into millions of fragments, the vapor escaping harmlessly into the atmosphere.

Faye stared down at it, then up at him. "You should have told me who you were," she admonished. "Of course, I probably wouldn't have believed you, so I would have had to—" She stopped talking as his right hand began to touch her body, first checking her necklace, then traveling along her arms, and back down her torso, causing a myriad of pleasant, unfamiliar sensations. "Wh-what are you doing," she stammered around her suddenly dry mouth.

"Making sure you don't have any more of that stuff on you."

"I don't," she assured him.

"I don't believe you." He twisted sideways, checking every inch of her.

By the time he'd finished, Faye was totally enamored with the responses his exploring had created. She made no effort to get away, and instead lay passively on the ground, her eyes closed, smiling to herself.

"*Stop it!*" he growled. "It won't work on me, and it looks bloody ridiculous on you!"

Faye opened her eyes. "What do you mean?"

"I mean there's no point in trying to look...alluring."

"Alluring." Faye rolled the word around on her tongue. "I'm not trying— Oh, *oh!*" As she spoke he slid to one side and rolled her onto her stomach, wrenching her arms behind her back. Her dress bunched up to her waist. He gave a furious exclamation and yanked it down. "If your lack of underwear was for my benefit, it was a wasted effort!"

Faye's euphoria dissipated as she felt his anger surround her, chilling her, frightening her. She gasped in a breath. "What are you doing?"

His voice wasn't at all friendly. "Taping your hands together."

"Wh-why?"

"Because I don't want to be knocked out cold and left in these woods overnight. Wasn't that your plan?"

Faye's eyes filled with tears as his grip became painful. Her face was pressed down into the dirt and leaves, and her light dress gave no protection from the dampness of the ground. She was wrong! He wasn't the Wizard, after all! Her entire body began to tremble at the implications.

"I'd probably die of exposure if I spent the night out here in this weather!" He picked up his backpack, stood and hauled her unsteadily to her feet. "Was that the idea?"

"N-no." Faye leaned against him for a moment to get her balance. He mustn't have liked it. He took a quick step sideways, and she half fell against the tree. It resisted her weight, and she staggered back.

"I bet!" Kent grabbed her arm. "Let's go." He turned in the direction he'd come from, practically dragging her with him.

"Where are we going?" she whispered.

"Denver."

"D-Denver? But I can't go like this. I—"

"You should have thought of that before you attacked me. Now you can bloody well freeze!"

"I—I'm sorry. I had to. You see—"

"You had to, did you?" His top lip curled up. "Well, I have to take you back to Denver." He paused, his snarl widening. "Where I will personally hand you over to Mr. Joseph Collingswood."

Faye stopped dead, certain all the blood in her body was draining to her feet. Her heart jumped around in her chest, and breathing hurt. "You can't do that," she gasped. "H-he'll ..."

"Cut out the frightened, helpless act!" Kent commanded. "I'm not falling for it again." He put a hand on her back and shoved. "You lead the way. I want to keep both eyes on you!"

Faye stumbled along on shaky legs, ashamed of her easy capitulation. She should put up a fight of some sort, she should do something. If only she wasn't such a coward! That's what she was—a total coward. She'd vowed to be brave this time, but she hadn't been. Maybe if she'd known he was the enemy, she would have been better prepared. Unwanted tears slid out of her eyes, blurring her vision. She blinked them away as best she could. It was difficult enough to be forced along like this, her arms bent behind her, while he breathed in short angry pants that increased her fright with each sound.

Now the forest was silent and the wispy fog billowed up around their ankles, almost to their knees. They walked for another five minutes before Faye risked a glance over her shoulder. Kent stared straight ahead, his face faintly flushed, his eyes malevolent blackness in his dark, satanic face.

Faye shuddered and whisked her head around, too late to see where her feet were going. A tree root snatched at her ankles. Before she smashed onto the ground, his arm was around her waist, holding her upright. "We'll never get out of here at this rate!" he snapped.

Faye turned to face him, her eyes widening as he pulled a knife from his pocket. She took one glance at the flash of steel, gave a terrorized whimper, and backed away, her retreat halted by a huge lodgepole pine.

Kent followed her gaze down to the knife, then looked up at her, appearing even more enraged. "What the hell do you think I'm going to do?" he shouted.

He moved one step toward her, then another. Her legs stopped providing support and she sank to the ground, bowing her head so her chin touched her chest, then completely fell apart. This was all so terrible. He wasn't the one she'd expected. He worked for the others. He'd drag her back to Denver, and turn her over to Collingswood. She knew exactly what would happen there. They'd demand the formula, and, when she refused to give it to them, they'd hurt her ever so badly. A vision rose in her mind of a similar scene, played out years ago. In spite of herself, she got caught up in it, her mouth opening and closing, her body trembling in silent, total terror.

"Oh, for Pete's sake!" He attempted to pull her up, but, although she didn't resist, she didn't make any effort to help. He let her sink back down to the ground, then knelt beside her. She cowered away from him, trying to make herself as small as possible. He put a hand on her shoulder and she jerked as if he'd burned her, twisting away, attempting to avoid looking at him as well as escape the horrific images flitting in and out of her consciousness. It didn't work. Scenes of another time returned with such intensity, they almost blocked him out. His hand cupped her chin, forcing her to face him. When she did, his features faded into the landscape of her mind, intermingling with the shadows there.

He swore quietly to himself. "Whatever you're expecting isn't going to happen." His voice softened. "Don't look at me like that, damn it. I'm not going to use this thing on you."

She released little murmurs of fright, wrenching her chin from his grasp. "It—it won't work," she told him, her words punctuated with frantic gasps for air. "I—I won't tell you. No matter what you do to me I won't tell you. You might as well kill me here, because I'll never, ever, tell."

His face paled to off-gray. "Kill you? I'm not going to kill you." He heaved a huge sigh, and lifted the knife. Faye attempted to crawl away from him into the cover of the bushes. He caught her arm, and his voice softened to soothing. "It's okay. I'm not going to hurt you. I swear I'm not. I just want to undo your hands."

She peeked at him from under her lashes, shuddered, and squeezed her eyelids tight, convinced he was tricking her; he was going to do something terrible to her, right out here in her forest.

"Keep still!" he ordered.

She couldn't; she was trembling too hard. He bent her forward against his chest, and leaned over her shoulder. A second later she felt the cold blade against the inside of her wrist. She bit her lip, tensing, trying to prepare herself. She wouldn't tell.... She wouldn't tell.... She ...

The tape loosened and ripped, freeing her wrists. Faye released an astonished whimper, dragged her cramped arms around, and buried her face in her hands, weeping helplessly into them.

"Damn!" Kent grumbled. He sat, resting his back against the tree beside them. "I didn't hurt you," he said in an aggravated tone. "At least, I didn't intend to. On the other hand, you've knocked me out—twice, in fact—and were quite prepared to do it again. You've also managed to frame me for grand larceny and convince the police I'm out of my mind. How come I'm the one who feels like Captain Hook?"

"I don't know," Faye said, weeping. "He—he was so much nicer."

"You flatter me," Kent replied with a sneer.

Faye risked a peek over her fingers. Kent's face had relaxed somewhat, although traces of that cold fury remained. She covered her eyes, quivering. There was a rustling sound, then something warm over her shoulders—his leather jacket, traces of his body heat captured inside, lingerings of his faintly exotic scent. She tried to shrug it off.

Kent groaned. "You'd rather freeze, wouldn't you?" He shifted closer, dragged her stiffly resisting body onto his lap, and wrapped his arms around her. "It's okay," he soothed. "It's okay. Calm down, now. No one's going to hurt you. It's okay." One of his hands began gently stroking her back as if she were a kitten, while he repeated the same words, over and over. "It's okay. Calm down, now. It's okay." After a few minutes, she gave up and relaxed into him, fighting to control herself. "You can stop crying now," he said tiredly. "If this is an act, you've sure convinced me."

She lifted her head from the nest of his shoulder to gasp a faint, "I'm...trying," before nestling back down. For about fifteen minutes they sat quietly, while Kent methodically stroked her until her terror abated.

He finally broke the silence. "I shouldn't have lost my temper," he admitted. "I'm usually a pretty calm person. I'm sure you find that hard to believe, but it's true. I certainly don't go around brutalizing pixies, or at least, I haven't before."

She felt his breath against her hair, while her ear, pressed against his chest, recorded steady, even heart-beats.

"You're still shaking," he said remorsefully. "You poor little thing, you're cold and wet and scared out of your mind." He patted her shoulder. "I'm not going to turn you over to Collingswood. I don't like him either. I wouldn't give him a dead cat, much less Tinker Bell."

She sighed with relief, gave one last shudder of a sob, and wiped her eyes with her fingers.

"That's better," he encouraged. He caught her hand, fingering the tape's red imprint on the pale skin of her wrists, his light touch sending tingles of awareness up her arm. "Will it bruise?"

She shook her head.

He dropped her hand. "Good. I didn't mean to frighten you like this. I just didn't want you to knock me out again."

She took a quick look at his face. Without the rage he was quite sweet looking, his dark eyes wide with anguished apology, his frown one of puzzlement. "I had to," she whispered. "I didn't know who you were."

"I'm Kent MacIntyre. I thought you might remember me."

She shook her head. "That's not what I mean. I didn't know you were the Wizard."

"Who's the Wizard?"

"A powerful magician," she explained. "He and I are going to fight the Alchemist."

"Ah." He shrugged a shoulder. "Sorry, I'm no Wizard, and I don't know any Alchemists."

She eyed him uncertainly. "You must be," she insisted. "The atomizer—"

"A stupid parlor trick," he interrupted. His cheekbones, under his tan, reddened.

"And my sleep spray didn't work on you."

"Not this time." He winced. "It did manage to give me a dreadful headache, though."

"Oh," said Faye. "I—I'm sorry."

"So am I," he agreed. "That's part of the reason I lost my temper, I guess, although I don't consider it a particularly good excuse." He sighed and shifted her off him onto the ground, wiping the last trace of moisture from her face with his thumb. "Are you okay now? Hmm?"

"Y-yes." She'd stopped trembling, although her breathing quivered the tiniest bit.

"If it's any consolation, I feel absolutely terrible. I've never seen anyone so terrified before." He shivered and rubbed his arms. "I hope I never do again."

The anguish on his face and in his voice persuaded her more than his words. She studied him, considering all the evidence. "Are you sure you aren't the Wizard?"

"I'm positive."

"Maybe you just don't want to tell me," she suggested. "Wizards like secrets."

"Wizards like secrets, do they? What are you, some sort of Wizard expert?"

"Sort of, I guess."

"I see." He buried his smile in the palm of a hand. "Exactly how many Wizards have you met?"

It was such a silly question, she had to laugh. The sound tinkled through the forest, somehow dispelling the gloom of the early evening. "None!" she gurgled. "There's not a whole bunch of them, you know."

"But one's going to show up soon?"

"That's right," she said, nodding. "I've been waiting for him."

"I'm afraid you'll have to keep on waiting, babe." He shook his head. "You don't live in the same world as the rest of us, do you? You'd probably get off the burglary charge by claiming temporary reality confusion." He sighed regretfully. "It's academic, anyway. I'm not capable of turning you over to the police."

"You aren't?"

"Unfortunately for me, no. Ah, well, the evidence against me is only circumstantial. Besides, I can always hot-foot it across to Canada and hope they don't extradite me. If worse comes to worst, perhaps prison is more fun than they let on." He passed a hand across his forehead. "I'll tell you what. You satisfy my curiosity about all this, and I'll forget I ever saw you."

"Really? You'd really do that?"

"Yes, I would." He turned his head from side to side and massaged a temple. "I'm probably being an idiot, but it won't be the first time I've been a sucker for a pretty face." His smile was forced and painful.

"Have you ever tried eating nuts?" Faye asked.

His jaw dropped. "Pardon me?"

"Nuts," she repeated. "Some Wizards have a problem with headaches. They have to eat nuts to counteract them. Peanuts work, but I believe macadamia nuts are best."

"Oh," said Kent faintly. He drew in a gasp as, for no particular reason, Faye slid her fingers into the pocket of his jacket, still resting on her shoulders.

He held both hands in front of him, palms facing her. "It doesn't mean a thing," he warned.

Faye held out a hand. "How do you do?" she inquired politely. "My name is Alfaye Merline. I'm so pleased you've finally come. Let's go to my place and make plans." She pulled out the package of macadamia nuts, handed it to him and smiled triumphantly.

Her Wizard had arrived.

4

"ACTUALLY, THERE ARE over twelve thousand species of ferns," Faye explained. "Of course, only three hundred and sixty of them grow naturally in this climate, but I've been experimenting—"

"Ferns?" Kent interrupted. "I thought you were talking about birds."

"I was," she said. "Now I'm talking about ferns. Don't you like them?"

"The ferns or the birds?"

She glanced up at him out of the corners of her silver-blue eyes. "You're making fun of me, aren't you?"

"I'm just trying to follow you. Let's see, you went from deer to elk to some flower called mule-ears...."

"That was at least two sentences ago. Now we're talking about ferns."

He chuckled into her earnest face. "The ferns are...stupendous. Go on."

She continued, and he listened with part of his mind, while the other part watched her in amazed disbelief. She definitely knew her way around this forest, and from the sound of things, she'd adopted every plant and animal in the area and was planning on bringing him up to speed.

She'd insisted he accompany her back to her cottage, refusing to tell him anything until they were warm and dry. It hadn't been that difficult to persuade him; he was much too curious. How had someone like her managed to plan a break-in at a place like Sharade Research? Why was she so terrified of Collingswood? What had she really taken, and for what purpose?

In spite of his denials, she appeared totally convinced that he was the mysterious Wizard she'd been waiting to meet. He had to admit he was responsible for some of that convincing—after all, he'd smashed that atomizer right in front of her. What on earth had he been thinking?

The delighted little sprite beside him was a welcome change to the one who had stared at him with horror-filled eyes only half an hour ago. That look would stay with him for a long time. He doubted he'd ever forgive himself for treating her so badly, for scaring her so much. He knew how volatile his temper could be. That's why he kept tight control on it, disguising his tendency toward violence with a flippant manner that few could depose. If he was going to lose it, did he have to do it with someone this helpless?

His self-disgust intensified when he felt a sharp mental query from Avril. He groaned aloud, although he should have expected it. Avril picked up strong emotions from him, no matter how far away she was. She knew he'd gone off the deep end; her concern was more for his victim than for him. He tried to calm her down, knowing that when he told her the details, she would rip into him with painful thoroughness. The idea made him wince, but he considered it due penance for the treatment he'd dished out to the vulnerable woman beside him.

"Here it is!" Faye announced happily as they stepped out of the woods into a small clearing.

The house was so much like what he'd imagined that Kent had to smile: red roof, brown logs, the front yard a mixture of brightly colored flowers and thick mossy grass. On one side stood a greenhouse and a couple of sheds that matched the house. The other side, and what he could see of the back, had been sectioned off into numerous square growing areas, each one filled with bushes, trees and flowers. Beside the greenhouse was the biggest, healthiest-looking garden he'd ever seen.

"I live here alone now," she said as they approached the structure. "After my father died, they told me I should move into the town, but I like it here."

"It's hardly a town," he observed. "There can't be more than a hundred people living there."

"A hundred people!" Her eyes widened. "Do you think there's that many?"

"Yes, I think there's that many."

"Oh." She paused. "Let's see, there's the Normstams, that's five. The Rawlings, that's three more...." She went on with the list, counting on her fingers. "I think you're right. There could be a hundred people in town."

"Oh, Lord," he muttered. "Where have you been all your life?"

"I told you. Here. Before that—" She shrugged enchantingly. "Well, there's a lot of before that, but I don't want to tell you right now."

"Why not? You've told me everything else."

"You haven't told me anything," she complained. "I'm ever so curious about you. I thought if I told you about me, you'd tell me about you."

"I'm not half as fascinating as you are," Kent declared.

She stopped outside the door, and brushed aside a strand of his hair. "I didn't know we'd meet under these circumstances. I'm sorry I tried to knock you out."

He shrugged. "Just don't do it again, hmm?"

"I wouldn't!" She pursed her mouth into a considering pout. "I'm so glad it's you. Did I tell you that? I am. I like you. I liked you the first time I met you."

"That's why you knocked me out?" he teased. "Because you liked me?"

"No. I had to, you know that." She arched up on her toes and touched a lighter-than-air kiss to his lips, her body pressed against his. His mind flashed the information that underneath that almost-transparent gray-brown dress, his pixie was totally naked. It took a great deal of willpower to gently push her aside. "I don't think we should do that."

"Why not?" Faye's silver-blue eyes widened to astonishment. "We are going to be lovers."

"Oh, no," Kent said, groaning. "Don't tell me Tinker Bell's a nymphomaniac!"

"I'm not a nymphomaniac," she retorted. "I'm a virgin."

Kent felt his face warm. "Do you announce this to everyone you meet?"

"No." She shook her head seriously. "Just you. You should know, shouldn't you?"

"I don't think it's any of my business."

"Of course, it is."

He looked down into her upturned face, her eyes iridescent, her face filled with excitement, anticipation. "It really isn't," he insisted, hoping she'd take the hint and drop the subject.

Her hand came up, a finger brushed across his lips. "We will be lovers, Kent MacIntyre." Her voice had a soft, high lilt, and her eyes had changed from frightened innocence to wily temptation. She waved her arm, forming a slow half-circle in the air. "We will be together. And together, we will be magic."

Kent ground the fingernails of his left hand into his palm. Her words and her motions seemed to cast a spell, creating a vision of them together, her small perfect body a white flame against his darkness. Together, they would be magic, her hands touching him, his caressing her....

"Stop it!" he ordered hoarsely.

The happiness on her face faded to bleakness. "Then our time together will be over, and then— Well, you know what happens then." She stared up into his face, as if pulling thoughts from his mind. "You do know?"

He opened his mouth, closed it again and dumbly shook his head, unable to think of a single thing to say.

"You don't? Oh, well, it's not important now, anyway." She drew in a breath and opened the door.

Kent rolled his eyes to the heavens, prayed for strength, and followed her inside.

They entered a square room that appeared to serve as a kitchen, eating and living area. The room was dominated by a large stone fireplace that covered half the length of one wall. In front of it was an oval braided rug, a long green sofa of questionable age, and a huge overstuffed gray chair. At the other end was the kitchen, complete with a white wooden table and matching chairs. Two doorways off the room showed a tiny bedroom and the bathroom. None of the furniture matched, but it all seemed to fit together in an unusual, unreal manner.

Most of the decor was provided by the plants. Every inch of almost every flat surface was covered with potted plants, all appearing incredibly healthy. The front window faced east, and in front of it were hanging pots filled with more plants. The entire place was permeated by a scent he immediately associated with her, although he couldn't remember smelling it before.

The table was set in readiness for two: forest green place mats, white plates, green mugs that matched the place mats, and old-fashioned cutlery. "Who's here?" Kent demanded.

"No one. Just us." She flitted into the room and stood in its center, pivoting gracefully. "What do you think?"

"Think?"

"Do you like it? I made a lot of it myself."

"It's...charming." He paced around, checking both the smaller rooms to make sure they were alone. When he came out of the bathroom, Faye was in the bedroom, the door wide open while she blithely removed her clothes.

Kent averted his eyes, deciding this was too darned tempting, and returned to the bathroom. Although her sweet little body had felt awfully good, and every time he touched her, his own body ached in response, Kent had no intention of carrying through with her suggestion that they become lovers. For one thing, she was a criminal. For another, taking advantage of someone that helplessly naive would leave him riddled with guilt.

"You're a vegetarian, aren't you?" Faye called out.

"Yes," he grunted absently. He made a face at his reflection in the bathroom mirror—he could use a shave, and perhaps a bar of soap. He did a mental run-through of the few items he'd stuffed into his backpack. None of them was a razor. Oh, well, he wouldn't be here long.

"I thought so. Tea?"

"What?" He reentered the room and did a perfect double take as he realized she was bustling about the kitchen, preparing a meal. "What on earth are you up to now?"

"You're hungry," she said with some exasperation. "You haven't eaten since this morning, have you?"

"No, but—"

"Then you should eat." She pulled a steaming dish from the oven of the woodstove, and set it on the table. "It's all ready."

"I'm not here to eat! I want to hear your story, and get back to civilization!"

"We can eat first," she said sunnily. "It's a vegetarian meal—I'm one, too." She pointed to a chair. "You sit there."

He didn't move for a moment, but when she settled herself down and gazed expectantly at him, he gave up. "Oh, fine." He sat down and took a cautious sip of the tea, a herbal affair hinting of cinnamon. "How come the table was set for two?"

She eyed him as if he'd lost his mind. "There's two of us. You and I."

"But it was set when we got here."

"Of course, it was." She filled his plate, then hers. "I got as much ready as I could beforehand. Don't you do that? It saves rushing around when there's company. You aren't really company, of course, but you haven't been here before, either."

Kent took a healthy slug of tea. "Gosh, Toto, I don't think we're in Kansas anymore," he muttered as he set down the cup and picked up a fork. He waited until she'd taken a few mouthfuls before concentrating on the meal, which tasted deliciously different.

"It's my mother's recipe," Faye explained. "One of my favorites."

"It's great," he assured her. "Listen, Faye, do you think you can put together one coherent thought and explain to me what you were doing at Sharade Research?"

"Not yet. It's a long story, so we should finish eating first. Besides, I've done all the talking. I want to know about you. I've never met a Wizard before, and I—"

"I told you, I'm not a Wizard!" Kent interrupted. "Right now, I'm a detective."

"But you're not always?" she guessed.

How could someone who appeared so totally out of touch have such wise eyes? "No," Kent admitted after a slight pause. "I also work with my sister—"

"Don't tell me," she interrupted. She rolled her eyes up to stare at the ceiling. "A month. Spring. Not May. April!"

"That's real close," he said, nodding. "Avril. How did you know?"

She laughed, wrinkling up her nose, not answering. "Go on. What do you do with Avril?"

"We own a company called VisTech. I used to help Avril run it, but I haven't had much to do with it for a couple of years. I've done more business consulting for other companies."

She nodded. "The day-to-day operations of a company wouldn't appeal to you, if everything was going smoothly."

Everyone, including Avril, had thought he was nuts when he announced he wanted out, yet this odd creature understood right away. "That's pretty much it. It's more of a challenge to go into a place with problems and try to set things straight."

"That makes sense," she agreed. "And for variety, you do this detective thing."

It wasn't exactly a question, but Kent found himself explaining. "Stuart Investigations is owned by a friend of mine, Dan Stuart. He claims he's getting too old for fieldwork, so I lend him a hand whenever he needs it."

"This Dan Stuart, is he your counselor?"

"My what?"

"Your counselor. Every Wizard is assigned a counselor when he's starting to develop his powers. The counselor provides advice and support, and is the only one who can control the Wizard."

Kent concentrated on his plate. She was dead accurate. He'd met Dan when he was in his early twenties, and Dan had immediately slid into the role of mentor, friend and adviser. Dan knew all about Kent's unique abilities, and was the one who had advised him to develop them as much as possible, and keep it to himself. Dan was the one who had encouraged him to leave VisTech and strike out on his own. And, although Dan lived in Denver, and Kent lived in Calgary, whenever Kent was getting that urgent, restless feeling, Dan called up with some interesting assignment.

"What about parents?" Faye asked right out of the blue.

Kent slowly raised his head. "They passed away several years ago."

"Mine are both gone, too." Faye's bottom lip pouted out sympathetically. "It's horrid, isn't it? What about your wife? She's still alive?"

"I imagine so. Divorce isn't fatal, although sometimes it seems like it will be." Kent set his fork down with undue care as he realized what she'd just asked. "How did you know about that?"

"About what? Your wife? I told you, I'm . . ."

"An expert on Wizards," he completed. "But . . ."

She ignored his puzzlement. "What happened?"

He was too stunned to understand the question. "Happened?"

"Your wife. What happened to her?"

"Nothing happened to her. We got divorced, that's all." He picked his fork up again.

She watched him eat. "Why?"

"We didn't want to be married anymore, at least not to each other."

"Oh!" Faye wiped her mouth neatly with a napkin. "I guess you didn't love her, then."

Kent didn't want to even think about his marriage, much less have it dissected by this unusual woman. "I don't . . ."

"Wizards seldom fall in love," Faye went on. "If they do, it's forever, so you couldn't have loved her. You might have thought you did—probably because your sister said you were. She wanted you to settle down, you were fond of the woman, and you couldn't think of a good reason not to do it."

A cold chill started at the base of Kent's spine and worked its way up. "Why do you ask me anything?" he muttered. "You seem to know the answers already."

She arched a silver-tipped eyebrow. "You are simply a typical Wizard—restless, easily bored, and difficult to understand. All the legends say so."

Both his sister and his ex-wife, Daphne, had described him that way, too. Of course, he hadn't told Daphne about his unusual abilities; never could think up the words to explain it to her. In the end, he was glad he hadn't, although sometimes he thought that if he'd been more honest, they could have salvaged something of their relationship. She'd ended up very hurt, and he'd ended up feeling like a first-class creep.

"You shouldn't have married one of the others," she told him. Her eyes were filled with age-old wisdom. "It only works in a few cases, and only if you're both willing to compromise." She patted his hand across the table. "My parents' marriage was like that."

"They were divorced?" Kent guessed.

"No, of course not." She sipped on her tea. "My father was one of the 'Others.' He was Welsh, but my mother was from Tir nan Og."

"Where on earth is that?"

Faye shook her head. "I have no idea. My mother left there to be with my father." She leaned forward, lowering her voice as if telling him an immense secret. "You can't go back, you know. That's why I've never been there."

Kent studied the green-tiled floor, fighting his twitching lips.

"She was one of the Ayaldwode," Faye went on in a normal voice. She scooped a forkful of carrots off her plate. "One of the keepers of the forest."

"Ah," said Kent. "I suppose you're one, as well."

"Well, of course!" Faye sounded a bit exasperated. "Not like my mother. She was a water nymph. I take after my grandmother. She was a wood sprite."

"A wood sprite," he echoed blankly.

Faye went on. "Even though I'm only part Ayaldwode, I inherit their responsibility. My mother was very clear on that."

"Was she?" He cleared his throat. "You're the last of the Ayaldwodes, then?"

"No!" She tilted her head to one side. "At least, I'm not supposed to be. I wasn't raised in Tir nan Og, so there are some things I don't know. My mother said that there were Ayaldwodes all around the world, trying to take care of the forests."

"In that case, they're not very effective," Kent declared. "All the great forests are in danger these days."

"I know." Faye sighed. "We are mortal, you know. Pollution and destruction of the forests kill us as easily as they destroy everything else." Her voice saddened. "Now, all we do is preserve what we can, with hopes for a better age, when man will again appreciate what nature has given him and help us take care of it."

Kent decided it was time to turn the conversation back to reality. "Your father—you mentioned he was Welsh?"

"He was, yes. He was a sweet, gentle man. Very kind, very clever. My mother heard of his work, and left Tir nan Og to help him."

Kent focused on the parts of her response he could understand. "What was your father's work?"

"He wanted to find a solution for the water-pollution problems of the world. He devoted his whole life to it. We all worked on it. Since my mother was a water nymph, she desperately wanted him to succeed. But he didn't. Actually, he made things worse." She sucked in her bottom lip. "He didn't realize what we'd done until it was too late."

"And what had you done?"

"It was a mistake," she whispered. "You have to understand that. It was a mistake. We didn't do it on purpose."

"All right," he agreed. He reached across the table to squeeze her hand. "I believe you."

"That's why I had to knock you out," she said as if it made sense. "I had to stop it. Not only for him, but for the rest of the world. You see that, don't you?" Her eyes widened in desperation. "I didn't want to hurt you. Even today, I didn't want to hurt you. I had no other choice."

Kent could see the panic overtaking her again. He turned her hand over, stroking her palm, lowering his voice to a soothing calm. "It's all right. Calm down. It's all right." He waited until her pulse had slowed to a fast normal before quizzing her further. "What was it your father was working on?"

"It's called the Mozelle formula. It's a substance that would dissolve the common pollutants in water."

"And it didn't work?"

"It did work!" she insisted. "Unfortunately, there was a side effect. The substance itself mutated to a poison."

Kent hissed in a breath. "That's a serious side effect, all right."

"It's worse than that." She swept her eyelashes down, watching her fingers twist around her fork. "The poison rose to the surface of the water. My father's intent was to have it dissolve, but that's not what happens. Instead, when the water is exposed to ultraviolet rays, the surface tension breaks." She lifted her eyelids. "It mutates to a poisonous vapor that kills all life around it. *All* life. Plants. Animals. Everything."

There wasn't a doubt in his mind that this part of her story was true. "Oh, wow!" he whispered.

"That's not all." She straightened her shoulders. "Then, it dissipates harmlessly."

Kent stared at her as the blood drained out of his face. "How much does it take?"

"It's very potent. A few drops will cause the effect."

"Let me see if I've got this straight. A few drops of this substance cleans the water, but then turns to a poisonous vapor that kills all life."

"In a radius based on the volume of water and the amount of Mozelle used," she put in. "In something the size of the Great Lakes, it could be thousands and thousands of miles."

"And then, it dissipates harmlessly?"

She nodded.

"Oh, Lord," he groaned. "The perfect weapon."

5

"THAT'S WHAT I'VE GOT so far," Kent concluded. He
held the phone with his shoulder and watched Faye tidy
her small kitchen.

Dan's whistle of astonishment flew along the phone
wires. "Alfaye Merline?" he asked. "She claims she's
Alfaye Merline?"

"That's right," Kent confirmed. "Why? Have you
heard of her?"

There was a long silence at the other end, then Dan's
voice. "Yeah, I've heard of her, all right." His sigh was
long and drawn out. "She disappeared about three
years ago, along with her father, Glendon."

"What?"

"That's right. Glendon Merline was a British chemist or something of that nature. Worked for the World
Environmental Agency. Don't remember much about
Alfaye. They were over here on some WEA assignment, and they just vanished. No sign of foul play,
nothing. One day he was there, the next day, he was
gone and so was she."

"My God!" Kent muttered.

"Exactly! There was some hue and cry about it, with
him being a British citizen and all. They scoured the

country for him, but neither of them were ever found."
Dan hesitated. "She says her father's dead now?"

"That's right. She said he had a heart attack last year."

"Well, well, isn't this fascinating," Dan mused. "Has she mentioned what she's been doing all this time?"

"Not yet."

"I wonder if this is all tied together with the Sharade break-in somehow. See what else you can find out about her."

"I will," Kent agreed. He paused. "Dan, there's no way I can turn her over to the police. She's just . . . too terrified. A day in jail would be the end of her."

There was silence at the other end of the phone. "Hopefully it won't come to that," Dan said finally. "Where are you tonight? Neverdale?"

"Sort of. I'm staying at Faye's place."

"Ah." Dan's voice was fraught with meaning. "Do you think that's wise?"

"It's wiser than trying to find my way through this forest in the dark."

"Uh-huh."

"Cut it out," Kent growled. "I'm sleeping on the sofa."

Dan chuckled. "That's a new name for it."

"Dan!"

"Okay, kid, whatever you say. Listen, can you get her to Salt Lake City tomorrow?"

"I'll try."

"Go to the Shamrock Motel out near the airport, and keep a low profile. I'll meet you there. And be careful, Kent. I haven't found out much about Collingswood, but I . . ." He paused. "There's something else going on here, but I haven't narrowed it down yet. I think you'd better get her away from there, though. I've got a bad feeling about this."

"Join the club," Kent grunted. "Okay. I'll see you tomorrow night."

"Right. Oh, and Kent . . ."

"Yeah?"

"Watch out for those sofas. If you aren't careful, you can create a bunch of tiny little love seats that call you Daddy." He was chuckling as Kent slammed down the receiver.

Faye slid a log into the fireplace, watched it catch, then drifted across the room to curl up in the middle of the sofa, her legs folded underneath her. "Are you all right?" she asked. "Did your headache come back?"

"Not yet." Kent sat in the big armchair and rested his forearms on his knees. "Will you come to Salt Lake City with me tomorrow? My friend, Dan, would like to meet you."

She looked pleased. "It would be a great honor to meet a Wizard's counselor. Besides, I'm your Ayaldwode. I have to stay with you."

"Uh-huh. Listen, are you the same Alfaye Merline who vanished with her father, Glendon, three years ago?"

She didn't seem to find the question at all surprising. "Yes," she said, nodding.

"Why?"

"We had to," she said earnestly. "We didn't know what else to do. That formula's a dangerous thing to know."

"You are the only one who knows about it, right?"

She lowered her eyes contritely and shook her head. "The Alchemist knows about it."

"The Alchemist?" Kent repeated. "Who's that?"

She lifted her gaze slowly and swallowed. "J-Joseph. Joseph Collingswood. He knows about Mozelle, and he has part of the formula."

"How did he get it?"

She pulled at the material of her dress, pleating it into neat rows. "He . . . stole it."

"Did he?" Kent had the impression that wasn't quite how it had happened. "How did he do that?"

"He was very clever," Faye said after a momentary pause. She stared at the fireplace, her eyes wide and distant.

"Why don't you start from the beginning," Kent suggested. "Your father, Glendon, worked for the World Environmental Agency, didn't he?"

She blinked her silver-blue eyes to focus on him. "Yes, he did. He was an expert on water pollution, and he spent a lot of time traveling, advising governments and private companies. When he wasn't doing that, he was doing research. One of his projects was Mozelle, but before it got very far, the funding for it was cut, and it was dropped. He was very disappointed, and decided to continue the work on his own time. We had a little lab in our house, and we did our own research there."

"How did he meet Collingswood?"

"He was sent to Sharade Research. There were some suggestions that Sharade had been dumping chemicals into the Colorado River— Sharade asked WEA to check into those allegations, and see what had to be done. The man in charge of the project was Joseph Collingswood."

"Oh."

"H-he didn't seem like a dangerous man, Kent. I never really liked him, but he was friendly enough at first." She shuddered. "He even invited us to his place for dinner a few times." Her eyes widened, and her breathing quickened.

Kent left the armchair to sit beside her, and she immediately snuggled into him, her hand on his thigh, her head on his shoulder, her breasts pressed into his side. Kent bit his lip against a surge of sexual desire, and stroked a soothing hand down her back. "Go on," he croaked. "I need to know this."

"Okay." She breathed into his neck as she lifted her head. "By the time we went to Colorado, my father had developed the first part of the Mozelle formula, and was searching for a way to dissipate the poisonous toxin harmlessly. He had a couple of ideas, and he tested them on water from the Colorado River." She paused and looked down at her hands. "That's when he accidentally stumbled on the vaporization technique."

"And he told Collingswood?" Kent guessed.

"No!" she said indignantly. "He didn't tell anyone, but one of the research assistants knew what he was working on—a young man named Arnold Livingston. Arnold didn't know the entire Mozelle formula, but he did know bits and pieces of it. Arnold told Joseph about it, and Joseph told my father there was a great deal of money to be made with a formula like that. Dad said he wasn't interested in money, and Joseph seemed to accept that. After the Sharade project ended, we went back to Britain."

"So why did you disappear?"

She sighed a long, trembling sigh. "Arnold," she whispered. "He was a nice sort. A sweet, rather vague fellow. He phoned us one night, and told us Joseph had been after him for the formula. He sounded scared. He warned us that we should be careful, that Joseph really wanted that information." She wiped at her face. "My father thought Arnold was overreacting. A week later, he tried to phone Arnold. That's when we found out that Arnold had been killed."

"Killed?" Kent said sharply. "How?"

"Horribly," she murmured. "His body was found in the river—he'd been . . . tortured. . . ." She took a gasping breath. "We didn't know what to do. Who would believe us? We had no evidence of anything. We destroyed all our research notes about Mozelle, anything we had about it." She lowered her voice, speaking so softly he had to bend his head to hear her. "A month or so later, Father was sent to Florida, to do some consulting work. He was already concerned about Joseph, about his interest in Mozelle, and he insisted that I come with him. One day, Joseph just showed up at the house we were renting. He knew details of Mozelle, and he tried to convince my father to give him the rest of the formula. When Father refused, Joseph threatened him. We were ... terrified."

"Okay," Kent soothed. He stroked her with his hand, feeling the delicate bones under his fingers.

"We ... decided to go into hiding. We were already in America, we had some money. We traveled around, and finally settled in Neverdale. It's remote enough that finding us would be difficult, and we could keep an eye on Joseph."

"How could you do that?"

She lowered her head and moved her hand down his thigh. "Arnold's uncle used to work at Sharade. He knew where we were and he kept us ... informed. He used to send us lists of projects—things he had access to."

Kent massaged the tense muscles at the back of her neck. "Who was Arnold's uncle?"

"Webster," she said. "His name was Webster Harrison, and he used to be head of security at Sharade Research."

"Head of security," Kent repeated pointedly. "But he just ..."

"Died," Faye completed. She looked up at him with overbright eyes. "That's right. He died a month ago." She cuddled closer. "Before he died, he told me that Joseph had begun some secret research at Sharade. He sent me all the information he could about it. I figured out what had been done and I . . . decided to break into the labs and change the experiment results. Webster flew to Salt Lake City, I met him there, and together we planned the break-in at the Sharade Research Lab. He was the one who got me that fake driver's license."

"Why did Webster need you?" Kent wondered. "He was security chief. He could have just done it."

"No, he didn't know enough."

"And what do you know that he doesn't?"

She tilted her head to one side and looked up at his face. "I worked a great deal with my father. Of course I naturally know a lot about chemistry, besides what I learned in university. I also took quite a few computer courses."

"You went to university?" Kent shook his head. "You couldn't possibly have. You're no more than a child."

Her chin jutted into the air. "I'm twenty-seven. I have two degrees in botanical research, and I would have had another if we hadn't . . . left."

"*You* have two degrees?"

"Yes." She laughed at his amazement, a sound that tinkled through her tiny house. "I'm only part Ayald-wode, Kent. The other half is Welsh."

"I must remember that. Okay, go on. Webster was going to help you break into Sharade."

"That's right. When I got to Denver, I discovered he had died." She gave Kent a sad look. "I don't believe it was a heart attack."

"I'm not sure I do, either."

"I didn't know what to do," she went on. "I didn't have the plans for the security system—Webster was going to help me with that part of it. I phoned the company and asked them who had taken over for him, and they told me Ron McAllister's name. They also told me he was going away. I thought he might have left his security badge at home, but when I went to his house there was a security system, and I couldn't get in. The little sign on the window said Stuart Investigations had installed it. I thought maybe they'd have the plans at the office, so I went there and . . ."

"And knocked me out," Kent finished for her.

"Exactly," she agreed. She watched the flames, then turned sad eyes toward him. "I didn't know who you were. Honestly, I didn't. I did ask, but you wouldn't tell me."

Kent squirmed uncomfortably. "Faye . . ."

Her gaze searched his face, her expression transforming to sparkling excitement. "Was it all part of your plan?"

"Plan?" Kent repeated. "Uh . . . what plan is this?"

"To defeat the Alchemist." Her fingers tightened around his thigh. "That's why you're here, Kent. You are my Wizard and you have the magic to defeat the Alchemist!"

"NO!" KENT INSISTED. "I really don't know anything about this. I am not this Wizard character, I don't know any magic, and I have no mysterious plan about defeating this Alchemist of yours."

"You just don't want to tell me," Faye muttered under her breath. She pulled a pillow and blanket from the small closet inside the bedroom, and sighed. This wasn't turning out at all the way she'd anticipated. Oh, she'd expected to have to explain a few things to the Wizard, but this one didn't seem to know much about anything. He must be fairly new at this. He didn't appear to believe her, he refused to share his secrets, and, to make matters worse, he insisted on sleeping on the sofa in the living room. Her mother had mentioned Wizards were devious. This one excelled at it!

She paused at the bedroom door. The fire was almost gone, the embers glowing faintly in the darkening room. Kent sat exactly where she'd left him, in the middle of the sofa, stroking a thumb around the curve of his jaw while he thought. The top two buttons of his brown cotton shirt were open, the black curling hair underneath an exact match of that on his forearms.

Faye had expected a Wizard to be an old man, or at least one a lot older than Kent. A young, attractive man was a welcome surprise, and her awareness of him was another bonus. Too bad he was being so stubborn.

Kent glanced up, and smiled. "Are those for me?"

"Yes." She set the blankets and pillow beside him. "I still don't see why you're sleeping out here. I already told you we were going to be lovers. I don't know why you're being so difficult about it."

"I don't want to incur the wrath of your Wizard," he said. Although his tone was very serious, his eyes held a hint of teasing. "I don't think he'd like to find me in bed with his . . . Ayaldwode."

"I'm *your* Ayaldwode." Faye sank down onto the floor in front of him, facing the fire. "You don't believe me, do you?" she asked as she watched the last embers fade.

"Oh, now, I wouldn't say that." His voice deepened, his fingers lightly touched her hair. "It is a lot to digest."

A tingle started in the strands of her hair and worked its way down to her toes. She moistened her lips with her tongue, and rested her head against his knee. "It doesn't matter," she said. "In the end it won't make any difference."

"You make it sound like I don't have any say in the matter."

"You don't." He was stroking her head, absently, as if he didn't know he was doing it. "You made your choice a long time ago," she went on, her voice soft and dreamy. "You could have chosen not to use your power, but you didn't." His hand stopped, then resumed. "No matter what, I'm glad you're here. Ayaldwodes are supposed to help a Wizard. We really aren't good at this kind of thing without one."

"Not good?" His tone was amused. "You managed to outwit the police, the security guards and me."

"Well, I am part Welsh," she reminded him. "Besides, I did have help."

"And a lot of drugs. What is that stuff you used on me, anyway?"

"A combination of things. The long-sleep powder had poppy and lysimachia stamen, dried, then treated with a solution my mother told me about. The short-sleep spray is different. It can be...painful." She glanced up at him. "Kent, I really didn't—"

"It's okay," he interrupted. "No matter whether I believe you or not, I'm convinced that you believe it."

They sat in comfortable silence for a few minutes, Kent's hand still on her head, his thoughts obviously far away. "What happened to your legs?" he asked suddenly.

Faye stiffened. "My legs?"

"Yes. When I... Out in woods, there... I saw your thighs."

"Oh." The injury was three years old now. Her body had done its best to repair the damage but the skin was wrinkled, puckered and scarred, and some traces of discoloration remained. Perhaps that was why he didn't want to sleep in her bed with her. "Acid," she explained briefly.

"It must have been painful," he said, his voice warm with concern. "What was it? How—"

Faye twisted around to kneel in front of him, putting a finger on his lips to silence him. "I don't like to talk about it," she said. She began to trace her finger around Kent's mouth, but he put a hand on her wrist to stop her. "Do you think it's repulsive?" she asked.

"Repulsive?" He shook his head, his eyes like rich, dark velvet. "There's nothing repulsive about you, babe."

She leaned forward to brush a light kiss across his lips. His arms came up around her, and he began to return the pressure. Then he groaned and gently pushed her back. "Are you sure you want to sleep out here?" she whispered.

He cleared his throat. "Not especially, but I'm going to."

"All right." She sighed, then rose up on her heels. "Remember, we will be lovers. When you're ready, I will be, too."

"Stop that!" He jumped to his feet, hauling her up with him. "I'm only human. I—"

"No, you're not," she interrupted. "We both know it, so you can stop pretending." She tinkled a laugh at the thunderous expression on his face. "Good night."

He was still staring after her as she scampered into the bedroom.

KENT WOKE UP TO THE sound of someone carefully making as much noise as possible. He opened his eyes and jerked to a sitting position, taking a couple of seconds to figure out where he was, and what was going on. Faye was flitting around the room, watering plants, talking to them, and moving them around. She picked up a clay flowerpot and set it down with an unnecessarily loud thump, then glanced over at him. "Good morning," she chirped. "Did I wake you up?"

"Wasn't that the idea?" he grumbled groggily. She wore a long brown skirt, a pale green, almost-transparent blouse and, judging from the way she moved, probably nothing else. "Don't you own any underwear?" he asked.

She gurgled a giggle. "Do you always wake up grumpy?"

"Always." He threw back the blankets, remembered he wasn't wearing much, and pulled them back up. "Can you leave the room, please, so I can get dressed?"

She put her hands on her hips, pursing her mouth as if considering it, then shrugged and went out the front door. Kent pulled on his jeans and his shirt and joined her.

It was just past eight o'clock. The sun was up, the sky bright blue but with heavy accumulations of white clouds, suggesting the possibility of later rain. Outside the cottage, nothing interesting was happening—flowers lifted their heads in the faint breeze, two deer grazed side by side at the edge of the forest. The deer glanced at them, then at each other and went back to eating. Faye looked anxiously around while Kent buttoned his shirt. "Do you hear anything?" she asked.

"No. Why?"

"I don't know. It's just . . ." She shrugged. "Probably nothing. I sometimes imagine things."

"No kidding," he drawled.

She lifted frosty-tipped lashes to glance up at him, the look in her silver-blue eyes both innocent and beckoning. "Did you sleep all right?" she asked in a throaty whisper.

"Splendid, thanks." His arm came up to encircle her shoulder, but when he realized what he was doing, he jerked away and went inside to the bathroom.

"Cut it out!" he ordered the reflection in the mirror. "She is one innocent young lady. Keep your hands off her!" The character in the glass leered back at him wickedly and he sighed.

If she hadn't announced she was a virgin, he would have spent the night with her. He'd like to think he was better than that, but the plain facts were, he wasn't—his marriage had proved that. He wasn't made for a commitment that involved settling down and being faithful forever. He was never again going to put himself in the position of actually being expected to do it. He spent time with any woman who came along, spelling out the rules very clearly beforehand. The charming creature outside with the tempting eyes was simply not capable of comprehending this. She was someone in trouble, someone he was going to help if he could; and that was that. *No hanky-panky, Mr. MacIntyre. Try to remember that!*

When he emerged she was in the kitchen, wringing her hands nervously. "It must have been my imagination," she told him. "I couldn't see anything."

Well, he could. He could see a good fifty percent of her body under that filmy shirt, and, although he made a great attempt to stop staring at it, it was almost impossible. He turned his back to her. "Do you think you could possibly find something else to wear before we leave?"

Faye glanced down at what she was wearing, then back up, her expression changing to one of amusement. "What's wrong with this?"

"It might rain," he hedged. "And it's rather cool out there."

"I'll wear a jacket." She wrinkled her nose at him. "Do you want something to eat first? Tea? Fruit?"

"That would be great. Thanks."

She flitted around the kitchen, putting on the kettle, pulling things out of the fridge. Kent had just finished gathering his things when he thought he heard something. He glanced at Faye, but she was involved in whatever she was brewing, humming to herself with a lilting sound that was as tempting as the look in her eyes. He resisted the urge to sing along with her and went out the front door.

At first he couldn't hear anything. Then he could— a deep, low throb. He struggled to place it, his heart pausing as he did so. A helicopter.

It could mean anything, he assured himself as he went back inside. They might not be coming here. If they were, he had a few tricks up his sleeve, and Faye had the sleeping powder. "I think we may be having company," he said as he closed the door behind him.

"Why? What's—" She froze with her hand on the door of the fridge. "What's that noise?" she whispered.

"A helicopter. It could be nothing, or . . ."

"Or it could be him." Her eyes reverted to panic. She darted to the closet in the back, pulled out a pale green jacket, and thrust her arms into it. She swung her brown woven bag around her neck. "Let's get away."

"Hang on," Kent soothed. "Don't panic. We can—"

Faye ignored him, rushed to the front door and pulled it open. As she did, the helicopter's thump-thump grew louder. "Stay inside," Kent hissed. "We—"

He was too late. Faye raced into the clearing, heading for the forest. Kent swore and started after her. The sound increased as a huge gray-and-blue egg-shaped helicopter materialized over the side of the hill, circling to block their path. Faye swerved toward him, her eyes wide with terror. Kent grabbed her hand as the chopper herded them toward the cottage. He dragged her back inside and slammed the door behind them. "Wait a minute. Let's find out—"

She yanked her hand from his grip and darted through the kitchen to open the back door. As Kent rushed after her, the front door splintered. "Stop!" a man's voice commanded.

Kent whirled around. A brutish-looking, wide-shouldered man had broken in the door, a gun clenched in his fist. "Don't move!" he warned. "Don't even think about it."

Kent snatched the pot of tea off the kitchen counter, hurled it into the man's face and raced out the back after Faye. She had skirted to the right, around the planting areas, and was just yards away from the bushes when a short, bulky man appeared from around the side of the house. Kent shouted a warning and Faye veered away—too late. The man took a running dive, landing on top of her. She went down with a high, shrill scream, just as a glancing blow to the side of Kent's head knocked him to the ground. He lay there, catching his breath, trying to keep calm.

The bulky man with Faye jumped to his feet, bringing her with him. He planted an arm around her, pinning her arms to her body, while his free hand pulled a revolver out of a shoulder holster. He aimed it at Faye's waist. "Don't try anything!" he warned.

She was in no condition to do anything of the sort. Her pupils were dilated with fright, her chest heaving in and out in large, desperate pants. Kent rubbed his aching temple and looked up at his own assailant, a large unfriendly looking fellow with a jagged cut above the eye where the teapot had caught him, and some angry red blotches from the scalding tea. He thrust a meaty hand down to drag Kent to his feet. "Who the hell are you?"

"Isn't that my line?" Kent gasped.

The fist that connected with Kent's mouth suggested the man didn't appreciate his sense of humor. Kent was in the grass again, wiping his mouth with the back of his hand, and gagging on the taste of his own blood.

"Take her to the 'copter, Davy," the man ordered. "I'll get rid of this asshole."

Faye screamed, struggling. Davy raised his gun hand, obviously intending to smash it into her skull.

Kent glared at the gun, it sprang out of Davy's hand, falling into the bushes. Davy swore and bent to retrieve it. Kent leapt up, smashing his hands down on the back of Davy's neck. As he crumpled, the other man pounced on Kent, driving a fist into his face, then dragging him to his feet to receive another blow.

Faye screamed again, but Kent was helpless against the attack, unable to concentrate while he was being pummeled. He drove a fist into his attacker's stomach, the man's grip on him loosened, and Kent twisted away. Out of the corner of his eye he saw Faye dash for the forest. Kent's attacker turned to follow, and Kent exploded into him, grabbing the man's head and bringing up his knee to meet it with jarring force. The man slid to the ground.

Kent watched him fall, snatched in a breath, then staggered after Faye, his mind foggy from the pounding he'd taken.

She ran so fast and so easily through the trees that he found it impossible to keep up with her. Finally he stopped, leaning against a tree trunk to catch his breath. She kept going. He shuddered in a few groaning breaths, holding them to listen. There was no sound of pursuit, but no sound of a helicopter taking off, either.

A few minutes later, the bushes rustled and Faye crept through them. By then, Kent was on the forest floor, his strength slowly returning. Faye knelt beside him. "Oh, Kent," she whispered. "Your face—it's a mess."

"It's not that great from this side, either," he whispered back. "Are you okay?"

"Yes." She twisted her fingers together. "Why did you let them get so close?"

"*Let* them? Babe, I didn't have much say in the matter."

"You could have zapped them down from the sky," she said. "You could have . . ."

"I can't zap someone down from the sky, at least not without a bazooka, and I don't normally carry one of those."

She bent her head, her shoulders drooping. "You really aren't the Wizard, are you?"

He drew in a breath. "Nope."

"I thought you were," she said. "I really thought you were."

"Well, I'm not." He pushed himself to his feet. "Let's get out of here."

Faye shook her head. "I can't."

"What do you mean, you can't?"

"I can't." She looked up at him, her face a study in disappointment. "I have to wait for the Wizard. If I'm not at my place, he won't know how to find me."

"If he's such a great Wizard, he'll figure it out," Kent muttered. "You can't go back there, Faye. We don't know how many men there are—there had to be at least three—neither of those goons looked capable of flying a helicopter. Someone's back there, and when those men come to, they'll follow us. We have to get to Neverdale before they catch us."

"The forest will protect me," she announced.

"It didn't do a great job earlier."

The slight breeze abruptly ceased, the plants and trees hushing to stillness. "Neither did you," said Faye.

There were a lot of things he could have said right then—pointed out how she had revealed their position by tearing off through the clearing, by dashing out the back door without a thought, by not being prepared, by panicking. He didn't. He sucked his lower lip in under his teeth, feeling the sting of the cut on it, and squinted up at the sky. "How much stuff do you have in the bag?"

"What? Oh, long-sleep powder. Quite a bit. Why?"

"Then you should be able to manage for a little while, as long as you stay away from your place. I'll go down to the town, call the police and tell them you were attacked. They'll come up here and do something." He turned on his heel and left her there, kneeling under a tree, waiting for the Wizard.

GOING BACK DOWN was a lot easier. For one thing, he didn't have the slight weight of his backpack; for another, the way seemed a lot clearer now, the trees parting as if anxious for his departure. He shouldered his way through them, annoyed with both her and himself. For a little time, there, he'd wanted to be the one she was waiting for. Damn her all to hell. What had she expected?

She'd be fine, he told himself. As long as she stayed in the trees, they'd never find her. She had enough long-sleep powder on her to knock out two men—if she didn't panic. Stupid woman, darting off like that. If she hadn't acted like such a fool, he wouldn't have had his good looks ruined by that creep with the fist the size of Kentucky. He fingered his jaw, knowing it probably looked just as bad as it felt.

His motorcycle was in the bushes where he'd hidden it not twenty-four hours ago, parked beside an old green pickup that he assumed belong to Faye. He shoved on his helmet, wincing when it touched the large bruise forming on his cheekbone. As he clapped down the visor, he heard the whop-whop of a helicopter. He watched the sky, waiting until it came into view, knowing he was hidden by the trees. It circled a couple of times, then slowly flew south. He sat on his bike until he couldn't hear the sound anymore, then roared down the dirt road in a cloud of dust.

Perhaps he should have anticipated danger, but he was too preoccupied by both his own dark thoughts and the reassuring concern from Avril. He suddenly—and desperately—wanted to see her. He had never felt so inadequate, which was ridiculous. He was not a prizefighter, but he'd done all right, considering the odds against him—and Faye hadn't been hurt.

He should have taken advantage of her tight little body last night, damn it, instead of worrying about being a gentleman! No, that wouldn't have been right—she obviously wasn't in full control of her faculties. An Ayaldwode! A Wizard! Pretty ridiculous.

He decided to call Avril as soon as he got to town, just to hear her voice. Although they could exchange feelings mentally, details were too difficult to transmit. He wanted to tell her the whole story, even if she did yell at him for bullying Faye and then leaving. No matter how angry she got, Avril was always on his side. Right now, an ally would be wonderful.

He took an outside corner too fast, skidded around the following inside one, braking as he rounded the craggy rock on his right where a gray-and-blue helicopter blocked the road. He swore, took a wide turn back the way he'd come, only to find a black sedan had pulled across the highway. To his right was sheer rock; to the left, a killing fall. Two men stepped out of the sedan, both aiming rifles in his direction. He circled back to the helicopter, where the same kind of scene awaited him.

He was trapped.

6

FAYE WATCHED KENT LEAVE, then crept back through the forest. She was annoyed with herself for believing he was the one, and annoyed with him for appearing so perfect. Last night, she'd been convinced he had power—this morning, he'd let those men beat him up, and almost hurt her. Kent was no Wizard. Good thing he hadn't spent the night with her, after all.

When she reached the edge of the clearing, she slid behind a cedar bush to survey the scene. Kent had been right about one thing—there were three men. They stood in a little group beside the helicopter, while one spoke into what appeared to be some sort of two-way radio. He finished his conversation. One man climbed into the helicopter, the blades began to spin, the machine rose, and, like an angry eagle, took off.

The two men left behind walked unsteadily into her cottage. Faye found a comfortable tree to lean against, and settled down to think. She was perfectly safe in the forest, she assured herself. They couldn't find her in here—they weren't even going to bother looking. Sooner or later, they'd leave, either because they were tired of hanging around, or because the Wizard had come. She didn't have to be scared. Still, she pulled her jacket tightly around her, hugging her bag for comfort.

She was sorry Kent wasn't the Wizard. He was so sweet, so nice looking, so attractive. Plus, he'd been company. She was lonely. She hadn't known she was lonely, but now she knew. She'd been locked up here too long; it was time she rejoined the world. She may be an Ayaldwode, but she was also part Welsh. That must be the part that missed the company of people. Maybe someday, it would be safe for her again. Too bad it wouldn't be with Kent.

For someone who wasn't a Wizard, he'd done some pretty amazing things. Okay, he'd gotten a bit beaten up in the process, but she hadn't been hurt. He'd taken a few punches for her, and most of those were entirely her fault—she was the one who had blindly panicked, raced around like an idiot, completely lost her ability to reason. She remembered the look on his face when she'd said he hadn't done a good job of protecting her—for one second, he'd looked as if she'd slapped him. She hadn't taken care of his face, either. She had been so preoccupied with the fact that he'd let himself get hurt, assuming that meant he wasn't the Wizard.

Right now, she didn't care if he was or wasn't. What difference did it make? She was sitting here, scared and all alone, when she could have been with Kent. She had just sent away a very kind man, one she found compellingly attractive, one who was willing to help her. She was tired of being alone, sick of waiting for some mythical being to show up and solve everything. When it came right down to it, she wanted it to be Kent.

One of the men came out of the cottage and peered up at the sky, holding a hand to shield his eyes. He began to walk in her direction. She slid away through the underbrush, her heart beating pitty-pats of fear. She hadn't expected them to come after her.

She found a new vantage point, decided to be prepared, and reached down for her bag. It wasn't there. She fought down the waves of panic; she knew she'd had that bag with her—she must have dropped it. She could find it. She crept very slowly back the way she'd come. When she saw the brown woven bag lying underneath a tree, she breathed a sigh of relief. She'd feel a lot safer with her long-sleep powder in her hand.

She watched carefully for five minutes—no one was about, the forest appeared deserted. The man must have returned to the cabin. She darted out, snatched the bag, and whirled to return. Something struck her shoulder with a sharp, painful rap. She fell, like a wounded deer, onto the forest floor.

KENT SURRENDERED. He didn't see many options, other than being shot to death on the road, and he didn't much care for that choice. He stopped about halfway between the sedan and the helicopter, parked the bike on the side of the road, and waited to see what they'd do next.

The two men in front of the helicopter came toward him. Both were over six feet; one a square hulk with blond hair, the other narrower, older and darker. They held their rifles expertly aimed at his belly. A glance over his shoulder showed the other two men approaching, prepared to shoot him in the back. "Keep your hands where I can see them!" ordered the blonde in front of him.

Kent raised his hands chest high, palms out. He could disarm them one by one, but that would give the others an excuse to shoot him—something he'd rather avoid. He'd have to wait for better odds, and a better opportunity. "I'm not armed," he called out. "What do you want?"

"FBI," Blondie announced. He hauled a black vinyl square from his jacket pocket, waved it around, and replaced it.

"FBI, eh?" Kent studied them. "What's up?"

"We'll ask the questions," Blondie said.

Kent grimaced as someone yanked his arms behind his back and snapped on a pair of handcuffs. Someone else tore off his helmet and patted him down for weapons, removing his wallet, his knife, and his package of macadamia nuts. All this time, at least two rifles were pointed at him, one from behind, one from in front. When the men were satisfied he wasn't armed, they stepped back.

Blondie flicked open Kent's wallet. "Ah," he said. "Kent MacIntyre. Good." He thumbed through the plastic sleeves, reading the contents. "You're a private detective?"

"That's right," Kent agreed. "You guys need me to help you out?"

The man's smile showed no amusement. He shoved the wallet into his own jacket pocket. "Where's the girl?"

Kent gave him a half grin. "I didn't know I was supposed to bring a date."

The man clenched his jaw. "I'd advise you to cooperate, Mr. MacIntyre. The FBI doesn't take kindly to your activities."

"They probably don't like yours, either," Kent retorted. "They hate people impersonating them. I believe they take it as a personal insult." The tension in Blondie's jaw increased, and Kent went on. "They also don't carry .308 Winchester hunting rifles, and don't have agents with IQ's under twelve." He paused, then added. "I believe that eliminates all of you."

Blondie lifted his right fist, smiled sweetly, and rammed it into Kent's stomach. Kent doubled over, gasping.

"Let's start again," Blondie suggested. He grabbed Kent's hair, pulling his head up. "Where's the girl?"

"What girl?"

The next blow was forestalled by the crackling of the radio on Blondie's belt. He let Kent's head fall, took a few paces away and unclipped the radio, speaking softly into it. He replaced it on his belt and returned. "They've got her up there," he announced. "Burton wants this idiot up there, too." He graced Kent with a malevolent grin. "He wants to deal with you personally."

Kent had a good idea what that meant, but he was more concerned with the first part of Blondie's statement. Was it a bluff, or could they possibly have got Faye? She was supposed to stay hidden in the forest. She had her long-sleep powder with her. They couldn't have got her.

Blondie turned to the man beside him. "Take Martin up with you to keep an eye on MacIntyre. Shertz and I will meet you at the airport in an hour."

The short, mean-faced man on Kent's right heaved a sigh. "Do I have to go in that damn thing?" he whined. "It makes me sick."

"Don't be a wimp!" Blondie said sharply. He grabbed Kent's arm, and gave him a shove. "Get in the chopper."

Kent staggered along between them, struggling to remain calm. If they really had Faye, he'd have to keep cool and think. If they didn't have her, he was still going to need all his faculties to outwit them.

Martin slid open the side door and climbed into the back, dragging Kent behind him. Kent flopped onto the bench seat, leaned his head back, and closed his eyes. He shouldn't have let Faye stay in that stupid forest, no matter how much she objected. He should have made her come with him. At least they'd have been together; he could have done something to keep her calm. His breathing rate increased as he imagined her terror. If they'd hurt her, or frightened her, by God, they'd suffer for it.

As the machine's motor started, Kent received a message of despairing concern from Avril. He spent a few moments in silent communication with her, bolstered by the intangible presence of her thoughts. He sent her a reassuring, *Don't worry, it's not that serious,* and pushed her away. He needed to concentrate.

The helicopter rose. Kent peeked from under his lashes at Martin, who was shifting uncomfortably from side to side, one hand on his stomach. Kent focused in on the man, sending him the suggestion that his stomach pain was intensifying. Martin's shifting increased, his facial color transformed from white to pale green.

Now, Kent considered the handcuffs, building a mental picture of them in his mind, then imagining them open. It worked. He slid them off as unobtrusively as possible, checking on his guard out of the corner of his eye. Martin appeared too concerned with his own sickness to take much notice.

It was a five-minute trip. Kent kept his hands behind him the whole time, his eyes closed while, one by one, he emptied his mind, forcing away the anxiety in his stomach, the ache of his jaw, and the gnawing concern about Faye. By the time the helicopter began its descent, he was ready.

The front door of Faye's cabin opened as soon as they landed. The man responsible for Kent's battered face stepped out, his demeanor that of triumph. He didn't appear to be armed, unless the set of brass knuckles on his right fist could be considered a weapon. He must be Burton, the one who wanted to "handle Kent personally."

Beside him was the brown-haired, square-nosed guy, whom Burton had referred to as Davy. Davy had a gun in his right hand, while his left arm supported a defeated, miserable-looking woman with silver-blond hair. It was Faye, with no jacket, and her blouse ripped half off her. Her hands were cuffed in front of her, her head lolling down, her shoulders drooping as she sagged against her captor.

Kent had never considered himself capable of purposefully injuring anyone. Now, as he watched the three figures start across the clearing, he realized he'd been wrong. He was quite willing, even anxious, to hurt those two men, to make sure they suffered at least as much as the pathetic little pixie obviously had.

"Get out!" Martin commanded.

Kent swung around to face his unwell companion. Martin's face was olive green now, the rifle he held swaying unsteadily. "Get out!" he repeated. "I'm going to—"

Kent silenced him with a quick jab to the jaw. Martin's head snapped back, banged against the window and lolled forward. Just as the pilot glanced back, Kent snatched up Martin's rifle and slammed the butt end into the pilot's temple. He, too, crumpled.

Kent snatched another pair of handcuffs out of Martin's pocket. Then he retrieved the pilot's rifle, holding it in his left hand, a finger on the trigger, while holding

Martin's in his right hand the opposite way. He allowed himself one second to draw in a long gulp of oxygen, then turned his body to face the door. It slid open.

"What the hell are you guys waiting for?" Burton demanded.

"You!" snapped Kent. He chopped the rifle butt straight into Burton's forehead, gratified by the crunch it made. Burton sank to his knees, hands over his face.

Behind him, only yards away, Davy had sized up the action. He swung Faye to shield half his body. "Hold it!" he yelled. "Drop those rifles, or I'll shoot her."

Faye stared at Kent as if she had never seen him before, her mouth opening and closing in total, uncomprehending terror. Kent focused on the gun aimed at her chest. It jumped from Davy's hand, vanishing into the tall grass. Davy stared at it, decided against trying to retrieve it, and took a step backward, dragging Faye with him.

"Let her go!" Kent shouted.

Davy eyed the rifle in Kent's left hand, and took another step backward. Faye sank almost to the ground. Kent bent his left index finger and squeezed the trigger. The bullet whizzed past Davy's right ear. He dropped Faye as if she were burning him, and stood dead still, his hands in the air.

"Get away from her!" Kent snarled. "Come over here!"

As the man began a slow walk toward him, Kent slid out of the helicopter and set down one rifle, while keeping the other trained on the two men. With his free hand, he pulled the two sets of handcuffs out of his pocket.

Davy took a dive at Kent, who rapped him sharply on the temple with the edge of the rifle. Davy fell sideways, landing in a groaning heap amid the grass and flowers.

Kent then handcuffed him to one of the leg supports of the helicopter, and Burton to another. He had no idea who had the key to the handcuffs, and he didn't much care. As far as he was concerned, they could spend the rest of their lives that way.

He glanced over his shoulder at Faye. She hadn't moved. She was still crouched in the grass, staring. He wasn't sure she had any idea what was happening. "You're okay, babe," he called back to her. "It's safe now."

She squeezed her eyes shut, shuddering. Kent did a quick check of his prisoners' pockets, relieving them of all their possessions. He did the same with the two unconscious men in the helicopter, removing the cartridges from the rifles and hurling the weapons into the forest. Finally, he unhooked the two-way radio from Burton's belt and smashed it with the heel of his boot. Then, with a gasp of a breath, he turned to Faye.

She was about ten yards away, staring up at him, the terrified silver-blue pools of her eyes accentuated by the mauve bruise that began on her left cheekbone and covered most of that side of her face. "K-Kent?" she whispered.

"Good guess." He put a hand under her elbows, pulling her to her feet, and shrugged off his jacket so he could use it to cover her. He kept one arm around her, and she sagged into him as he glared at her handcuffs, undoing them as he had his. "Which one of our friends hit you?"

"The . . . big . . . one."

Kent glanced at the helicopter, and the figures beside it. "Did he do anything else?"

"My . . . shirt." She stared down at the tatters. "They were going to . . . He . . ." She was breathing fast, panting and sobbing, her body shaking. As soon as she was free she twisted into him, pressing her face against his chest, her arms around his waist. "Oh, Kent . . . Kent, thank you. Thank you. . . I was so scared. I thought you were gone. I thought they would. . . And then . . . But I . . ."

She went on sobbing incoherent explanations while he held her as tightly as he could, murmuring, "It's okay, babe, it's okay now." When she made no sign of stopping, he picked her up and carried her into the cabin. She kept her arms around him the whole time, her small body quivering, her heartbeat fast and irregular. Kent sat on the sofa with her in his lap, cuddling her close, stroking her back, whispering soothingly into her ear.

It took a good ten minutes for her shudderings to subside, five more for them to be gone. She lifted her head, and put a hand on his cheek. "Oh, Kent," she murmured. "How did you get here?"

"I hitched a ride with Mug-Shot Airways. Are you all right?"

"I . . . I think so."

"Good." He lifted her off him and set her on the sofa, while he tried the phone. It had been ripped out of the wall. He swore and returned to sit beside her. "You can't stay here. Those men . . ."

She bowed her head, took a shuddering breath, then threw herself against him again, curling her arms around his neck. "I'm sorry. Please don't leave me again. I'm sorry. I want to come with you. I'm sorry." She punctuated each sentence with a slew of kisses, all over his face. "I'm scared. I don't want to be alone. Please don't leave me here."

"I'm not leaving you here," he mumbled. "I shouldn't have left you before."

"It was my fault. I'm sorry."

"It's okay." He regretfully unwound her arms and pushed her down. "What happened? I thought you were going to stay hidden until the police showed up."

Her top teeth slid into her lower lip, she swept her eyelids down, then raised them in a sheepish manner. "You were right," she admitted. "The forest didn't do a good job of protecting me."

He motioned with his head toward the front, wincing as he felt the first pangs of the familiar headache. "What did those fellows want? Did they say anything?"

"They wanted the formula." She waved a slender arm, shuddering again. "They thought I might have something hidden in here."

For the first time, Kent noticed that the place was a total mess—books, plants, chair cushions strewn all over the floor.

"They asked me where it was," she whispered. "When I wouldn't tell them, they... That big man, he..." Her eyes filled up again.

"I get the picture," Kent said grimly. "Do you know who they work for?"

"Probably Col-Collingswood, but they didn't say."

He patted her shoulder and stood. "You stay here for a minute. I'll be right back."

"What are..."

He ignored her, thrust his hands in his pockets, and went outside. The scene was exactly as he'd left it—no one inside the helicopter moving, the two men beside it groggily murmuring to each other. Kent stopped in front of them, and they stared up at him, Burton's battered face indicating plottings of revenge, Davy's looking more apprehensive.

Kent studied the helicopter, then looked down. "What do you want with her?" he asked mildly.

Burton gave a painful snort. "Since you're such a smart-ass, you figure it out!"

Kent squinted up at the sky. "Who hired you?"

"Co—" Davy started. Burton elbowed him and he subsided.

It was enough. "Joseph Collingswood?" Kent guessed. "What does he want?"

Burton shook his head, but Davy was willing to talk. "She took a formula from him. We were supposed to get it, and take her back to him. That's all. We didn't hurt her. We—"

"I saw her face," Kent interrupted. "Looks hurt to me." He motioned at Burton's manacled wrist. "That the hand you hit her with?"

Barton sneered up at him defiantly. "She's lucky that's all she got. Stupid bitch wouldn't tell us anything. I wouldn't have hit her if she had cooperated." He lowered his voice, baring his teeth into a savage grin. "She wouldn't say anything. Not a word, not even when I slapped her. But when I ripped off her shirt, she did. She screamed." He laughed. "Screamed and screamed all the time I was telling her what I was going to do. I had to hit her again to make her stop."

The sunshine had been warm, but now it felt cold— a cold that seeped through Kent's bones as he pictured the scene Burton was describing. He crouched down, leaning back on his heels, stroking a thumb over the curve of his jaw. "You like screaming, do you?" he asked softly. He focused on the metal circle around Burton's wrist, imagining it smaller, and smaller still.

Burton's eyes widened, and he clawed at his trapped hand. "What are you doing?" he gurgled. "How are you doing that?" Then, as Kent kept it up, he begged, "Stop it, damn you!"

Kent released the pressure, Burton sagged back, and Kent started it again.

Burton gulped in desperation. "You'll cut off my hand if you... Damn, that's what you want, you..." He went on with a graphic description of Kent, his voice getting hoarser, his face losing what little color it had. He wrestled with the handcuffs, shouted another obscenity, then screamed—a huge sound of agony that ripped across the clearing, echoing against the cabin and returning to them.

Kent slowly released the pressure. Burton massaged his wrist under the handcuffs, his face twisted with pain. "Keep your hands to yourself," Kent warned. "If there's a next time, you'll lose a lot more than your hand." He hissed in a breath through his teeth, rose and strode back to the cabin, knowing that if he stayed near the man one moment longer, he'd do permanent damage.

Faye was picking up knocked-over plants, crooning to them. He was pleased to see that some of the color had returned to her face, and she was breathing almost normally. He sank down on the sofa and she came to sit beside him. "What was that?" she asked.

"Someone apologizing for what they did to you."

"Oh," said Faye in a very tiny voice, her eyes full of questions.

"They do work for Collingswood," Kent told her. He looked around, thinking. "How far to your nearest neighbor?"

"Wentworths are about fifteen miles toward town. Taggerts are about the same distance the other way."

"Do these Taggerts have a telephone?"

"I imagine so."

"Can we get there without going on the road?"

"Of course. We'll have to cross the river, that's the only problem. It's not difficult, but it's a lot farther than on the road."

Kent considered the situation. The blond man who'd captured him on the road had mentioned a rendezvous in an hour. When the goons outside didn't show up, Blondie and friends would somehow get up here to see what was going on. It wouldn't take them long to figure out that Faye and Kent had run off.

There was a good chance that Blondie had more men at his disposal. If he had any sense, he'd deploy some of them to watch the road into town, and use others to search from the sky. The best thing for Kent and Faye to do was to stay in the forest, where spotting them from a helicopter would be difficult.

There was one major problem with that. Already Kent could feel himself weakening. He'd overused his special abilities today. In about forty minutes it would hit him, hard. When it did, he'd have to send Faye on ahead, and catch up with her later. In the meantime, there was no point in worrying her with it.

"We'll go through the forest to Taggerts," he announced. "I'm sure this crowd will expect us to go toward town. We're going to have to be real careful— these folks have friends who are going to start getting nervous soon. Can you change clothes into something more suitable for a hike?"

"All right." She reached around and patted his pockets. "Where are your nuts?"

"My what? Oh, my macadamia nuts. They took them when they caught me."

"They caught you?" She looked astonished. "I thought you caught them."

"That's not how it started."

Faye's forehead furrowed with puzzlement, but she didn't ask anything. She glanced around the room, retrieved her woven bag from the kitchen table, and brought it back to the sofa with her. "What are you doing?" Kent asked.

"Fixing your face." She pulled out a small glass jar, and knelt on the sofa. "Sit still," she ordered as she gently dabbed on ointment. It was cool, and felt wonderful against the soreness of his skin.

"What is that?" he mumbled, enjoying her light, soothing touch.

"It's my mother's recipe. Aloe vera, crushed rose petals . . . a few other things." She completed her task. "There. That should feel better."

"It does," he agreed. "Thanks."

She quivered in a breath. "Those men out there, are they hurt?"

"Not badly enough," Kent grunted savagely. He watched Faye slide to her feet, tiptoe to the still-open front door, and peek out.

She returned to him. "You'll have to come with me."

"Come where?"

Faye gestured toward the helicopter. "Out there." She picked up his right hand and tugged. "Please. I can't go by myself. I just can't."

He didn't move, his jaw falling open as he realized what she wanted to do. "Leave them!" he ordered. "You can't possibly want to . . ."

"I have to see how badly they're hurt." She rubbed at her eyes with one finger. "I'm an Ayaldwode. This is my forest. It's my responsibility."

"No. They're not seriously injured. They'll be fine. Leave them."

"Please, Kent. I have to. Please."

"Oh, hell, I don't believe this. They didn't give a damn about you, Faye."

She fluttered her lashes at him, her mouth closing to a pout. "Please."

Kent rolled his eyes and let her drag him to his feet. She slipped her hand inside his, wrapping her fingers tightly around his palm. "You are absolutely insane," he muttered as she led him outside.

She thrust her chin in the air and walked determinedly toward the helicopter. The two handcuffed men slid back as far as they could, eyeing Kent with wary apprehension. Faye's steps faltered as she took in the sight—two men, each a good four inches taller than Kent, handcuffed to the helicopter; Burton's forehead had one large bruise, and Davy's temple was about the same.

Faye stopped and looked up at Kent, her eyes as big as the helicopter itself. "Wh-what did you do to them?"

Kent rubbed a palm along his temple. "Asked them to leave us alone."

"Oh." She took three steps toward the men, studied them intently, then returned. "Take off the handcuffs."

"I don't think so." He caught her hand, intending to take her back into the cabin.

She resisted. "You have to take off the handcuffs. That one man—" she pointed at Burton "—there's something wrong with his hand. It's swelling."

"So's your face."

"Oh, but Kent . . ."

He shook his head, bunching his jaw into a stubborn knot.

Faye looked uncertainly from him to the two men, her forehead creased with worry. "I can't leave them like this."

Kent put a hand on each of her shoulders and turned her to face the cabin. "No."

She took two reluctant steps, and stopped. "They're hurt. They won't do anything to us."

Kent folded his arms over his chest. "Those are two very dangerous dudes, babe. If they're free, they'll do everything they can think of to hang on to you and get the formula. Do you want that?"

She shook her head no.

"Then leave them be."

He strode past her, but she skipped up beside, pulling his arm. "I still have some long-sleep powder left. I could put them to sleep."

Kent looked down into her upturned, frowning face. He knew a losing battle when he saw one. Faye wasn't going to give up; she'd simply keep at him until he capitulated. He tried one last, petulant attempt: "I don't have the key for the handcuffs."

She batted silver-flecked eyelashes at him.

"All right, all right. Put them to sleep, and I'll undo the handcuffs."

Faye ran into the cabin, returning with her bag. She filled her palm with dust from it, crept as close as she dared, and blew it onto the men, one at a time. As soon as they were asleep, she gave Kent an expectant look. He focused on the handcuffs, squeezing his eyes against the throbbing of his head. "There. I hope you're happy now."

She smiled up at him, not at all fazed by what he'd just done, and rose on tiptoe to kiss his cheek. "You're a darling."

"Uh-huh," he grunted. His cheek tingled where she'd kissed it, and her soft words were much too pleasing. He watched her apply ointment to both men's bruises, and to Burton's injured hand. "Can we go now?"

"No." She glanced up at him with anxious eyes. "I have to check the men in the helicopter."

He didn't even try to talk her out of it. "Hurry up, then."

She repeated the same process on those two, blowing her sleep dust on them even though they were unconscious, then doing her thing with the ointment. Finally she returned to Kent, and smiled with relief. "I'm finished. We can go."

Kent followed her back to the cabin, shaking his head in amazement. Once inside, Faye went straight to the kitchen and began fumbling through cupboards. Kent found his backpack and started gathering his possessions.

He was leaning against the fireplace, rolling up his sweater, when Faye approached him. "Here," she said, handing him a dish. "These should help your headache. They aren't as strong as macadamia, but I think Wizards—"

"I thought we'd settled that Wizard business," he interrupted.

"I made a mistake." She lowered her head with a contrite sigh. "It does happen. After all, I am part Welsh."

"Part Welsh," Kent murmured. She was standing too close, the angle of her head endearingly sweet, everything about her so gentle and kind. How could anyone possibly hurt her?

Kent set down the dish, slipped a hand behind her neck into the silky smoothness of her hair, and tipped her head up. Very slowly and methodically he bent toward her, his mouth laying an onslaught of kisses on her bottom lip, then pouncing when she moaned and opened her mouth. She tasted like pinecones and sunshine; her lips unbelievably soft, her whimpers of pleasure intoxicating. As her arms encircled his neck, he lifted her off the floor, needing to get as close to her as possible. She cooperated enthusiastically, sliding her sweet-smelling body against his as if they'd been doing this for years. He lifted his head, then filled his mouth with her again. One of her hands went into his hair, the other caressed his neck.

Kent raised his head, feeling his heart beating with unnecessary force. He pressed his lips together to hold in her lingering taste.

Faye's eyelids fluttered open. "Oh, my," she said in an approving half-whisper. "You should have kissed me like that before. I would have known for sure you were the Wizard."

Kent pressed a thumb pad to her bottom lip. "I'm no Wizard, honey."

She flicked out her tongue, touching it to his thumb. "You can't trick me again," she said, lifting her chin into the air. "I'm part Ayaldwode. I can tell a Wizard when I kiss one."

7

"I HAVE TO STOP FOR a minute," Kent announced. He leaned a shoulder against a tree, his breathing deep and ragged. "Can you hear anyone coming?"

"No," said Faye. "Sit down."

He slid down the length of the tree, bent his knees and rested his forehead on them. Faye sat down beside him, pulled a flask of water out of her bag, and wrapped his fingers around it. He took a tiny sip, handed it back, and let his head fall forward again.

Faye studied him, concerned. They hadn't been walking for any more than an hour, heading west along the side of the hill. It wasn't a difficult hike, yet with each step they took, she could see Kent's strength waning. Whatever he had done back there had drained his power. The forest rejuvenated her, but it was not having the same effect on him. He needed to rest, to eat, and to sleep. Even now, his naturally dark skin was paling, and the bruises on it looked angrier than ever.

He lifted his head and passed a hand over his face. "Let's keep going."

Faye shook her head. "Let's just . . . sit here for a minute."

He pressed his head back against the tree, and closed his eyes. "You don't need to rest. You could run all day through here, couldn't you?"

"I don't know," she hedged. "I've never tried it."

He chuckled, the sound quiet and weak in the silence of the forest. "You're so small," he mused. "Yet you're strong as a horse." He opened one eye to look at her. "No, make that a team of horses."

"Horses," Faye repeated thoughtfully. Now there was a good idea. "Can you ride one?" she asked.

"A horse? Yep. I worked on a ranch for a year or so. For the first six months, I could hardly walk, but after that I got used to it."

Faye turned her head to face the forest, and softly crooned the special words. Kent made a move to rise, and she put a hand on his arm. "Not yet. Please."

He settled back, hid a yawn behind his hand, and closed his eyes again.

"What was a Wizard doing on a ranch?" Faye asked. She wanted to keep him here, resting, as long as she could.

"Business consultant," he corrected. "It was ten years ago now, I guess. I wasn't anything more than a ranch hand then."

"And a Wizard," she added.

His lips twitched. "I keep telling you, I'm not a Wizard."

Faye picked up a pinecone to study it. "I saw what you did with those handcuffs."

"Oh, that!" He dismissed it with a gesture. "It's nothing. I've just got a strong magnetic field, that's all."

"A strong magnetic field?"

"Yeah. Some people are born that way. My cousin was much better at it than I am. Before he passed away, he taught me how to focus so I could move objects. He could move things without even being near them. I'm getting better at that, but I usually have to see or feel what I want to move."

"Telekinesis," Faye exclaimed, impressed. "Wow!"

He gave her a sexy, sideways glance. "See. No magic."

Faye set the pinecone down. "Depends what you consider magic. Everything I can do is explainable, but I know it's magic."

"And what is it that you can do?"

"Sleep potions, healing potions, growing potions—all the things a wood sprite knows. They're mostly things I learned from my mother and my grandmother."

He arched an eyebrow. "I thought you'd never met your grandmother."

"Oh, I haven't," she admitted. "But I can communicate with her."

"You can, can you?" Kent sounded skeptical. "How do you do that?"

"I don't do it. Grandma does it, when she wants me to know something. It's sort of hard to explain—it just happens. It's not at all like you and your sister."

Kent hissed in a breath and his eyes jumped open. "My sister?" he repeated, the words slow and questioning.

"Yes." She studied his reaction. "Isn't that what you were doing a few minutes ago? Telling your sister you were all right?"

"How could you possibly know about that?" Kent asked, his eyes and his voice showing his astonishment.

Faye didn't understand his surprise. "Is it a secret or something?"

"It's not exactly a secret. It's just . . . not common knowledge. Most people don't understand mental telepathy."

"I'm not most people," Faye reminded him. "I'm an Ayaldwode. We know these things."

"Ah." Kent closed his eyes again.

"Why can't you tell Avril to call the police?" Faye asked.

"It doesn't work that way. From this distance we can only exchange feelings. When we're closer, we can be a bit more specific, but it's not like talking to someone on the phone. Besides, do you really think the police would believe it if some woman from Canada called them up and told them to go rescue her brother in Idaho?"

"Probably not."

"Me neither." He slowly shook his head. "I think she'll call Dan, though, hopefully before he leaves for Salt Lake City. I don't expect we're going to get there today, and Dan gets awful cranky when I'm not where I'm supposed to be."

She considered this unique ability. "It must be nice to always be in touch with someone who cares about you. You'd never be alone."

"That's true. On the other hand, having someone tell you how you feel isn't all it's cracked up to be."

There was a hidden meaning in his words, one Faye had no problem picking up. "Ah," she said. "Avril thought you were in love enough to get married, didn't she?"

"Oh, yes." His voice sounded as worn-out as he looked. "She wanted the marriage a lot more than I did. Wanted me to settle down, but . . ."

"I know." Faye put her head on his shoulder. "Too restless, right?"

"Right."

"That's just typical Wizard behavior," Faye assured him.

"I told you, I'm not . . ." He let his voice trail off into a sigh, and rested his head against hers. "Never mind."

They sat there quietly for a few minutes, while Faye thought. "I know what's wrong with you," she exclaimed. "You've drained your magnetic field. You need to reestablish it, somehow."

"Uh-huh. And how do you suggest I do that?"

"I'm not sure," Faye admitted. "I should know how. I'll give it some thought."

He patted her shoulder. "You do that, babe. In the meantime, it might be best if you—" The bushes rustled, there were noises of an approaching presence. Kent was on his feet, his hand pulling her to a stand.

"It's nothing," Faye told him. "Just some . . . assistance."

He stared at her as if she'd lost her mind. "Assistance?"

"The horses." She swept out her arm, and as she did, two horses slipped through the bushes: a gray mare, and a chestnut gelding with a blond mane. They stopped when they saw Faye, and stood side by side, waiting.

Kent squeezed his eyes closed, then opened them again. "Horses," he said faintly. "Where did . . . ?"

"They belong to Mr. Taggert." She patted each horse, whispered into their ears, and smiled. "They don't mind helping."

"Horses," Kent repeated.

"You said you knew how to ride."

"I do, but how did you . . . ?" He stopped and shook his head. "Never mind. I know. You're an Ayaldwode."

"Part Welsh," she corrected. "You can ride the mare. Kalli, here, is a bit . . . crabby. He doesn't like his sister bossing him around."

"I can sympathize." Kent ran a long-fingered hand down the withers of the mare.

Faye was entranced by the gesture. She watched it, feeling an exciting warmth start in her abdomen, then spread throughout the rest of her body. Kent flicked his eyes in her direction. To her astonishment he blushed.

The color darkened his cheekbones, making him look almost healthy. She tore her gaze away from him. "The mare is callèd Katlin."

Kent held his hand flat against Katlin's nostrils, letting her catch his scent while Faye moved to the side of the gelding, put her hands on his withers and vaulted on.

Kent looked up at her, his eyes dark with wonder. Then he wrapped his left hand in the mare's mane and gave a lithe leap onto her back. "Lead on," he said.

Faye leaned over Kalli's mane and whispered their destination. The horse turned and began to amble back the way it had come. Faye crouched low to avoid the branches, checking behind her to make sure Kent was doing the same thing. As she saw his long, lean body pressed against the mare's back, the warmth that had begun earlier intensified. Her breath caught in her throat. Kent raised his head, and for one second she saw a reflection of her own emotion in his face.

The gelding faked a stumble. Faye turned her attention to where they were going.

THE RAIN BEGAN forty-five minutes later. It didn't start out as a drizzle, but rather the clouds opened up and dumped their entire contents in huge drops so thickly clumped together that seeing was difficult. It wasn't comfortable to ride through, but Faye was grateful for nature's camouflage. She wasn't sure if Kent had picked up the sound, but she'd heard it—the noise of a helicopter, about fifteen minutes before the rain started.

The four sleeping men they'd left at her place were getting assistance. Pretty soon, someone would be searching for her and Kent.

She glanced over her shoulder at him, and bit her lip. They'd come out of the forest fifteen minutes ago, and could now sit upright, but Kent wasn't doing that. His head was bent down against the rain, chin touching his chest, and his shoulders drooped with fatigue. A half hour ahead of them was a fork of the river. It would swell up fast in this deluge of rain, making crossing difficult. They could easily be trapped on this side of it.

That idea made her heart take a giant, frightened leap. *Stop it!* she told herself. *Stay calm. Don't panic.* She took another look at Kent, and dug her fingernails into her palm. She was his Ayaldwode; it was her responsibility to take care of him, to keep them safe. She should be able to do that—they were in her territory now, not some dark basement, nasty laboratory, or frightening city. In this weather, they would have difficulty using their technology to come after them. There were no roads back here, no access other than foot, or horse. She was certain none of those men were capable of using either of those means.

What would they do? Well, it didn't take a genius to figure out that she and Kent would have to get help. If they weren't on the road, it was natural to assume that they were in the back country, and would head for a neighbor's. If she were a bad guy, she'd simply go to the neighbor's and wait. She shuddered at that idea. Perhaps she was leading her Wizard right into a trap.

She forced herself to breathe deeply. A trap wasn't a trap until you were in it. Fully rested and prepared, she was confident Kent could handle anything, although, in this condition, he wasn't much of a threat. What she needed to do was find someplace where he could get himself together.

A gust of wind blew against them, and her horse suddenly stopped, then veered east. Faye was about to turn him back, but reconsidered. She hadn't been out this way for quite some time. There was something out here she should remember. What was it?

As they moved along the valley, it came to her. This part of the river was sometimes used by a tour company, for white-water rafters. A couple of years ago, the company had received permission from Mr. Taggert to build a small hut out here, in case of emergencies. She could remember how Mr. Taggert had considered the whole enterprise silly, and how he claimed to have made big money from the tour company for the use of the land. Somewhere around here, well back from the river, was that hut. It would be the perfect place to rest.

It took her and the horses a good while to find it. She wasn't sure of its exact location, and the horses didn't appear certain, either. A couple of times they had to backtrack, but Kent didn't notice, although once he roused himself to give her a confused, puzzled look. After that, he seemed content to let the horse take him wherever she wanted. At last, settled in the bushes to look as natural as possible, she found the green-and-brown prefab hut she'd been looking for.

The horses stopped in front of it. Their sudden lack of movement seemed to jar Kent awake, and he glanced around, shaking the rain out of his face. "Is this your neighbor's place?"

"Not exactly." Faye slid down to try the door—it was both locked and padlocked. She felt around in her bag, and found the small glass tube containing the remainder of the acid she had used on the locks at Sharade Research. There wasn't much left, but it was enough to dissolve both the padlock and the door handle. She breathed a thankful sigh, as Kent came up behind her.

"What's going on?" he mumbled. "What are we doing here? I thought we . . ."

"I—I thought we should get out of the rain," Faye explained. She looked at him anxiously—perhaps she should have checked with him before coming here.

"Good idea," he said, nodding. He glanced back in the direction of the horses, but they had wandered up to take shelter among the trees. He gave half a shrug and followed her inside.

It was a storage hut more than anything else—one square room occupied almost entirely by four padlocked metal lockers placed against one side and along the far wall. When they closed the door, the room was pitch-black. Faye left it open a crack, and checked her tube of acid. "There's not enough left," she said to Kent. "Can you open those locks?"

"I don't know." He sat down in the middle of the room, crossed his legs and closed his eyes. For a few minutes she didn't think he had enough strength left, then, at last the padlocks popped open, one by one.

"I hope that's all you need." Kent mumbled. "I don't think I can do that again for a while. Where is this place?"

"Out here," Faye said absently. She skipped around, checking the locker contents. Blankets, foam pads, bottled water, a container of kerosene, a small heater and a lamp. Kent lit both while Faye spread out the foam pads and arranged blankets. He was still strong enough for modesty—he turned his back while she pulled off her wet clothes and wrapped herself in a blanket. Then he made her turn away while he stripped. When he let her turn around, he was sitting on one of the foam pads, under a blanket. "This was a brilliant idea," he enthused. "I'm soaked."

He was, too, although he'd made an attempt to dry off. His hair was attractively mussed, and the muscles of his arms shimmered in the faint light of the lantern. Faye sat down on the other pad, feeling her body warm from the inside as she looked at him. "I'm not sure we could get across the river in all this rain," she told him rather breathlessly. "We might have to stay here until the rain stops."

"Where exactly is here?"

"We're a bit off-course. We're about halfway between Taggert's place and mine. The only real access to here is by the river. That's why the place is here. It's an emergency hut for one of those white-water rafting tours they bring down from MacKay. I'd forgotten it was here."

Kent's brow furrowed. "That's not very far. Those men . . ."

"The rain should make it difficult for them." She folded up a corner of the blanket, then straightened it. "I was thinking . . . um . . . if I were one of those men, I'd go straight to the neighbor's and wait. For us, I mean."

"I didn't think of that." Kent hid a yawn behind his palm. "You're right. That's what they'd do. We'll have to be careful when we approach Taggert's place. Real careful."

"I thought it might be better if you rested," Faye went on. "I mean, your magnetic field . . ."

"Is worn-out," he agreed. He patted her hand. "You're one clever lady. I could sure use some sleep, although I'm not sure it's wise."

"It's okay," she soothed. "I'll know if someone is coming."

"Good thing." He flicked a finger down her palm. "I sure won't. Let's get some rest, then come up with a plan before we tackle that crowd again."

Faye tingled more from his touch than from his praise. He must have felt it, as well. He bent toward her and kissed her mouth, softly and gently, nothing more. As she parted her lips under his, he groaned and moved away.

"What's wrong?" Faye asked. She put her head to one side. "I told you we were going to be lovers, and . . ."

"And I don't go around molesting pixies. It's the first thing they tell you in Wizard school. Keep your hands off the pixies, or you get turned into a toad." He lay down and pulled his blanket up to his chin.

"I thought you said you weren't a Wizard."

He closed his eyes, his lips twitching into a smile. "I thought you said I was."

"You're a Wizard, all right." Faye stretched out a hand and turned off the lantern, darkening their surroundings to almost-total blackness. "You're just an . . . inhibited one. I guess that can happen, although it's not what I expected."

"I don't know what you're expecting," Kent said, his voice sleepy. "That's part of the problem. You're one sexy little lady, and I'd certainly like to comply with your wishes. It just wouldn't be right."

"Why not?"

She heard him shift around. "I was married once, babe. It was big mistake—one I have no intention of repeating, in any form. I am simply not good at commitment."

Faye wasn't quite sure what he was getting at. "What's that got to do with . . . ?" Then it struck her. "Oh!" she exclaimed. "You think I want to *marry* you?"

He yawned again. "Not marriage, maybe, but if you've waited all this time before being with a man, it's only logical to assume that you've got something permanent in mind."

Faye was incredibly insulted that he thought her so foolish. "I certainly don't!" she retorted. "Wizards are terrible at long-term commitment. No one with any sense wants to be married to one. They're restless and easily bored and—"

"It's okay," Kent interrupted. "You've convinced me you're the leading Wizard expert in the room."

Faye could hear his amusement, and was unaccountably annoyed by it. He had rescued her, she was ever-so-grateful, and she thought he was marvelous. On the other hand, he kept acting like she was a mental case, and refused to allow them to become lovers. She lay down and pulled the blanket up to her chin. "They're also supposed to have strong libidos," she muttered. "Although, I guess that isn't true in all cases."

Kent's breath hissed out. "Where did you learn all this about Wizards?" There was an unusual tone in his voice; not anger, but a hint of warning.

"M-my mother," Faye stuttered.

"Perhaps she should have advised you not to torment one when he's tired."

"She did," Faye told him. "Not even Ayaldwodes always follow their mother's advice."

The warning note in Kent's voice darkened. "In this case, it might be wise to do so."

It sounded like more than a suggestion. Faye decided to take her mother's advice. She retreated over onto her side, and closed her eyes.

WHEN SHE AWOKE IT WAS still raining, and Kent was still asleep. She fumbled in the blackness to light the lamp, then slipped outside to peer at the cloud-covered night

sky, and to get a feel for the time. It was just after eight
o'clock, she decided. She'd been asleep for about six
hours. She drank some water, ate some dried beans,
and huddled back under the blanket to think. There
was no point in waking up Kent. They couldn't go
anywhere in the pouring rain. They might as well wait
until morning, since he wasn't about to do anything
more than lie around.

She lay on her side and watched Kent sleep. His jaw
was heavily stubbled now, his lips slightly parted. The
blanket only half covered his bare chest, the crisp curls
wickedly enticing. She felt that unusual warmth begin
again inside her, and turned away from him. She'd told
him they were to be lovers, and he hadn't done much
about it, other than kiss her. He was one weird Wizard, all right.

All that stupid talk about being married—what was
that? She knew how it was with a Wizard. She knew
they had no talent for futures and commitment, and she
certainly knew better than to fall in love with one. Her
mother had warned her about that. All she wanted was
to defeat the Alchemist, and to do that, they had to become lovers. Now that he was here, and they had this
opportunity, she was anxious to get on with it. It was
supposed to be a relatively painless experience. She was
certain Kent could make the magic happen, and then it
would be behind her.

Kent shifted over, making a little grunting snore. Faye
touched her fingertips to her lips, remembering the way
his mouth felt on hers, and that ache inside her began

again. She wanted this to happen, she wanted it to happen with him, and it was her responsibility to make sure it happened. However, he'd made it clear he wasn't going to cooperate. What was she supposed to do now? What on earth could be wrong with him?

Perhaps something unforeseen had happened. That was a possibility. Accidents did happen to Wizards, and he was a rather unprepared one. Perhaps there was more to this failed marriage of his than he was telling her. She sat up and eyed him uncertainly. He looked physically all right, but then again, she hadn't seen all of him, had she? He'd made certain she turned away while he undressed earlier. And, this morning, he'd had her leave the room before he got up. Perhaps, just perhaps, he was being so difficult because he had a physical problem that meant he couldn't . . . function. She lay back down, then sat up again. If she just moved his blanket a bit, she could easily check out the situation without him knowing. Under the circumstances, that might be the best thing to do.

THERE WAS A COLD BREEZE on his leg. Kent grunted and rolled over, but the breeze persisted, dragging him away from the very suggestive dream he'd been enjoying. He opened one eye, realized he must still be asleep, and closed it again. He was not awake, he assured himself, and little Miss Tinker Bell was not, repeat, not, studying his body as if she were his personal physician. This was a dream, and if it wasn't, it had exactly five seconds to turn into one.

The blanket settled back over him. Kent peeked from under an eyelid again. Totally naked, Faye was sitting on the foam pad beside him, legs crossed, elbows on knees, chin supported by her palms, her expression a mixture of confusion and relief. Kent stopped breathing as his chest tightened with unexpected emotion. She was so darn sweet, so incredibly well put together—her pink-tipped breasts, her white skin, that pale blond triangle of curls . . . His body responded at once, and his annoyance, and all his good intentions slipped away. She'd made it clear what she wanted, and he wanted it, as well. Fighting it seemed pointless.

He rolled over onto his back and opened his eyes. "Hi, babe," he drawled. "Whatcha up to?"

She jumped back, and he thrust out a lazy hand, catching hold of her ankle. "Don't run off, now."

She swallowed nervously, glanced down at his hand, then directly into his face. "I . . . um . . . didn't mean to wake you up."

"Uh-huh. What did you mean to do?"

"Um . . ." Her entire body blushed, a fascinating, enticing effect. "I'm . . . um . . . I was . . . f-finding out if . . . um . . . there was a problem."

"A problem?" he repeated. "What sort of problem?"

She swept her eyelids down, declining to answer.

Kent sat up slowly, and took her hand, massaging the palm with a finger. "What sort of problem?"

"A . . . a physical problem."

Kent pressed his lips together to control his smile. "A physical problem, eh?"

She nodded, her breath catching as he slid his hand into her hair, holding her head for his kiss. He rubbed his lips over hers until her mouth opened, then slid his tongue inside, tasting her soft moistness. When he raised his head, her eyes were dazed and beckoning, and her color had deepened. "Go on," he encouraged. "What's all this about a physical problem?"

Her face was about one inch from his, and the pulse in her throat raced nervously. "It doesn't matter," she whispered. "There doesn't appear to be one."

"I'm pleased to hear that." He put a hand on each of her arms, slowly stroking upward across her shoulders, then down to brush across the tops of her breasts. "Can I interest you in a demonstration?"

Her pink tongue slipped out to moisten her bottom lip. "A dem-demonstration?"

"That's right." He cupped her breasts in his palms, touching his thumbs to the hardening tips, watching the telltale pulse in her neck throb with reaction. He bent to press his lips against it, and she kept very still, except for one slight shudder. He rested his forehead against hers and looked her straight in the eye. "Do you still want to make love?"

Her lips trembled into a smile as she nodded.

"You're sure, now?"

Again, she nodded.

"If you really are a virgin, there could be some . . . discomfort."

"I really am a virgin," she whispered. "I want to make love with you, Kent. It's inevitable."

"You won't be sorry later?"

She pressed a small, scented palm to his lips. "I'm not going to be sorry—ever."

"All right." He kissed her again, but when her mouth opened under his, he resisted the invitation. It would be too easy to get caught up in his own passion, to forget that this was her first time, and accidentally hurt her. She made tiny purring sounds, wound her arms up around him, pulling him closer, pressing her breasts against his bare chest. He caressed the softness of her bare back, then gently pressed her down beside him. Her silver-blue eyes half opened to gaze trustingly up at him. He watched her expression as he stroked her breasts, taking great delight in her pleasure.

"Am I supposed to feel like this?" she gasped.

"I don't know." He circled her lips with his tongue. "How do you feel?"

"W-wonderful," she gurgled. Her back arched, and he responded to the invitation with his lips, tugging gently on each eager nipple. She tasted like nothing he'd ever tasted before, yet it was totally familiar, and he couldn't get enough of it.

Faye made little cooing sounds, urging him on, whispering soft words of pleasure at each touch. Kent was absolutely enamored by her reaction. He explored every inch of her with his hands and mouth, fascinated by the look of his dark flesh over her pale skin, and enjoying her taste, her scent. When he slowly parted her thighs and stroked the silky flesh between, her entire body trembled. She tossed her head restlessly from side

to side, murmuring his name. He moved to kiss her, and
her fingers danced over the muscles in his back, her
touch feather-light, yet scorching. "Oh, please, Kent,"
she moaned.

"What do you need, honey?" he said softly. He slid
a finger inside her. "This?"

"Yes, oh, yes."

She was moist and warm and definitely ready. He
knelt between her legs and gathered her hips up to meet
his. Then, with a slowness he found almost painful, he
moved into her.

She gasped and her eyes flew open. "Am I hurting
you?" he whispered.

"Yes, b-but I l-like it."

Her trembling honesty was as appealing as the in-
credible sensation of being inside her. He ran his hands
through her hair, caressing her delicate little ears, her
cheeks, her lips. She gazed up at him with absolute trust
and adoration, her eyelids flickering down as he cau-
tiously began to move. She buried her face into his
shoulder, while her palms pushed against his buttocks,
urging him on. He became lost in it, forgetting about
hurting her as he gave in to the demands of his own
body. She breathed his name into his ear, whispering
pleasure and encouragement.

Together, as she had foretold, they were magic.

"SEE!" FAYE MURMURED, her tone both sleepy and tri-
umphant. "I told you there would be magic."

Kent patted her shoulder indulgently. "So you did," he agreed. If she wanted to call it magic, she could go right ahead and do it. In the dim light of the little hut, with the wind hushing sighs around them, with her soft body pressed against him, the air itself seemed to tingle, and it was almost possible to believe she was right. "Go to sleep now," Kent encouraged. "You're not supposed to talk after making love."

She leaned up on an elbow to look at him, her brow slightly furrowed, her eyes still hinting of wonder. "Why not?"

"Because it always turns into either a performance review or a motivational dissertation, either of which usually leads to some kind of argument. It's better all around if everyone just shuts up."

"It's a strange custom, but okay." Faye brushed a kiss over his cheek, slid away from him and threw back the edge of the blanket.

Kent reached out a hand to hold on to her. "Where are you going?"

"Back to my own bed."

He snuggled her down against him. "Rule number two—you have to spend the night. It's rude to run off."

"All right." She slid over to flick off the lantern and rolled onto her side, with her back to him. "Good night."

"Not like that!" he said, exasperated. "You're supposed to cuddle. Get back here!"

"There sure are a lot of rules no one tells you about," Faye said with a sigh. She slid over and rested her silver-blond head on his chest.

Kent held Faye close in the pitch-blackness of the hut, smiling to himself. He usually enjoyed sex, but with her it had been an almost-mystical experience. It was probably because it was her first time, he reasoned. The wonder and enjoyment she'd felt had been transmitted to him. "Are you all right?" he asked after a few minutes. "I didn't hurt you, did I?"

"Oh, no!" she breathed. "I feel . . . marvelous."

"Good," he muttered. The pleasure in her voice assuaged the slight twinge of guilt he felt at taking her virginity. She'd wanted it to happen as much as he had, and it didn't sound like she was going to have any regrets in the future. Unless . . . He had another thought—one he should have had before—and groaned. "Faye?"

"Hmm?"

"We . . . uh . . . weren't what you'd call careful, here. Is there any chance . . . ?"

She yawned, her breath fluttering against his chest. "Don't worry about that. We won't have a child together."

Kent found it hard to believe that Faye had given the matter even one second of consideration. "Are Ayaldwodes in charge of conception, as well?"

"No, but you are."

"Oh really? Exactly how does that work?"

"A Wizard can't procreate unless he wills it," she muttered sleepily.

"Gee, I wish I'd known before that I was above the laws of nature."

She patted his chest with one of her soft little hands. "You aren't above the laws of nature, you work with them."

"Uh-huh."

"You didn't have any children with your wife, did you?"

"No." They had considered it, but he'd known from the beginning that it was a mistake, and wasn't about to compound the problem by bringing a child into the equation. Daphne had taken birth-control pills, or at least she'd said she had. He'd never actually seen them, but . . . No, he was letting Faye's imaginings get to him. "We were only married for a year," he added.

He heard her smile. "It only takes once."

"True. And we've just . . ."

"It's sweet of you to be concerned, but there's really no need." Faye moved her head, catching a strand of hair in his stubbled chin. "Listen, the rain has stopped. We'll be able to cross the river in a few hours. Good night, Kent." She gave a final, light yawn and relaxed into sleep.

Kent wasn't one bit tired. As a matter of fact, he felt strong enough to mentally lift the hut and everything in it. That was unusual enough in itself—he'd expected it to take a good twenty-four hours before he had most of his strength back. Good thing it hadn't—they had a few obstacles to overcome before they were out of this mess. Still, he was confident that as soon as they got to a phone, as soon as he could talk to Dan, most of their problems would be solved. Dan would know the best course of action to take to get Collingswood out of the picture.

He felt too good to worry about it now. Faye released a sleepy little purr and snuggled closer, her hand trailing over his chest. Kent closed his eyes and relaxed into unfamiliar contentment. Not only did he feel sexually satisfied, he also felt somehow emotionally soothed.

About twenty minutes later, he opened his eyes. His sense of well-being remained, but there was another sensation there, and Faye was directly responsible. Her leg was tangled up with his own, and her hand had drifted lower—now resting just below his abdomen, and threatening to drift even lower. The sensation was much too arousing to allow sleep. He waited another ten minutes. She was sound asleep—it would be a shame to wake her. Then again, he'd been sound asleep before she'd decided to play doctor. Besides, even if he knew he wasn't a Wizard, she certainly thought he was. He had the honor of the Wizards to uphold!

He shifted her limp form and stretched out above her. "Wake up, honey," he encouraged as he nibbled on her shoulder.

She partly lifted her lashes, her eyes underneath filled with sleep and confusion. "Why?"

He gave her a deep, slow kiss, then began tasting his way down. "We have to finish our discussion."

She gasped short, whimpering pants of pleasure. "Wh-what are we discussing?"

He caressed her thighs, pressing his lips to the puckered flesh of her scars. "Libidos."

"L-libidos?"

"That's right." He used his fingers to part her moist, velvet opening, then used his mouth and his tongue, while his thumb searched through the blond curls. She squirmed, arching and making soft moaning sounds of astonishment and pleasure. When he figured she'd pretty much lost the drift of the conversation, he slid up to straddle her, gazing down into her heavy-lidded eyes. "Libidos," he reminded her. He put a hand on each breast, tormenting the hard little tips. "You were saying . . ."

Her lashes fluttered down. "I shouldn't have mentioned that."

"Oh, but you did." He took her hand and guided her fingers to close around him. "What was that you were saying about mine?"

Her mouth opened, her eyelids flashed up, her expression that of delicious temptation. "Wizards have . . . uh . . . strong libidos," she murmured. Her tongue licked her lips. "I . . . uh . . . guess I was right."

Then her palms slid up his chest to clutch his neck, pulling him down to her. Softly murmuring endearments, she drew her legs up to encircle his waist, and as he joined with her, Kent could feel the magic again.

8

FAYE TOOK A LAST, regretful look around the interior of the little hut. The first weak rays of early dawn crept through the open doorway, giving the room a rosy glow. All the items they'd used had been carefully put away, leaving nothing but a lingering tingle in the air to indicate that they had ever been here at all.

That didn't matter, Faye assured herself. She'd remember last night for the rest of her life. After all, who could forget being with a Wizard? She picked up her bag from the floor, pausing in mid-motion as another snippet of Wizard information crossed her mind. Her mother had mentioned something. Did it mean . . . ?

Kent's lean figure blocked the light, covering her with his faint shadow. "Come on," he urged. "Let's get out of here before those bozos in the helicopter get their brain cells activated."

Faye slowly followed him out, shivering in the chilly breeze that greeted her. Kent pulled the door closed behind them and studied the lock. He looked terrific this morning, his hair slightly curling in the dampness, the bruises on his face subsided, his jaw almost bearded. He had on the same clothes—brown cotton shirt, well-worn jeans, and his leather jacket. An aura of power hovered around him, indicating that whatever had been wrong with his magnetic field had been repaired. It would be impossible to forget someone like this. Wouldn't it?

Kent dropped the lock and shook his head. "Your acid did a good job on this. I can't fix it." He stepped back from the hut and examined the small white sign on the side. "I'll settle up with these guys after we return to civilization." He grinned widely. "Better yet, I'll let Dan handle it. He's good at making stuff like this sound perfectly natural."

One of the horses gave an impatient snort. Faye turned to pat Katlin's warm nose and reached out a hand toward Kalli. He tossed his head away with an arrogant swing of his blond mane, and pawed the ground. "He wants you to ride him this morning," Faye explained as Kent came up beside her.

Kent nodded gravely at the horse, the dimple on his chin twitching slightly. "I'm flattered."

"So is he," Faye murmured absently. She chewed on her lip as she watched him settle the backpack on his shoulders. "Kent?"

He adjusted a strap. "Uh-huh?"

"I . . . uh . . . I will remember it, won't I?"

"Remember what?" he grunted, as he fiddled with the other strap.

Faye gestured toward the hut. "Being here with you. I'll remember it?"

"I'd like to think so." He tested the set of the backpack with a shrug of his shoulders. "Any particular reason why you wouldn't?"

"I just don't know if it works both ways," she explained. "I never thought to ask, and . . ."

Kent performed a slow-motion turn to face her, his dark, narrow-eyed gaze roaming her body. "You don't know if what works both ways?"

Faye had a sudden suspicion she shouldn't have asked. "It's okay. I . . ."

"No, no. Go on." He folded his arms across his chest. "I can't wait to hear this one."

Faye swallowed with a now dry mouth. "Well . . . um . . . my mother mentioned that a Wizard usually forgets all about his amorous encounters. I just . . . ah . . . wondered if that meant I'd . . . um . . . forget it, too."

"I see." Kent sucked in his breath and bent his head to examine his right thumb. "And you figure I share this charming character trait, do you?"

It had never occurred to her that he might not. "Uh . . . well . . ."

His head came up, the amber flecks in his eyes glinting in the early-morning sun. "I take it that's a yes?"

"You are a Wizard," Faye said apologetically. "Naturally, I thought . . ."

"That's enough of this Wizard nonsense!" Kent growled. He wrapped his fingers around her forearms and gave her a slight shake. "We must be up to Wizard insult number two hundred and twelve by now!"

"Kent . . ."

"And for your information, little Miss Wizard Expert, I am not, repeat *not*, going to forget I slept with you! *Ever!*"

"But . . ."

"Instead of filling your head with fairy tales, your mother should have told you not to climb into bed with someone you figured would act that way!"

"But it was you," she reminded him. "You . . ."

"I know it was me, thank you! My memory is working just fine! That is not the point!" He lowered his head until it was an inch from her own and glared into her face. "You do not go around sleeping with men who don't care enough about you to remember they've done it!"

Faye's bottom lip started to tremble. "I thought you did care about me."

"Of course, I do! What kind of a creep do you think I am?" His scowl grew fierce. "Scratch that. I've already got a pretty clear picture!"

"I don't think you're a creep," Faye said indignantly. She tried a tentative smile. "And I care about you, too. That's why I want to remember it."

Kent's scowl drained away, leaving a dark tenderness in his eyes and his voice. "In that case, I can't think of a single reason why you wouldn't."

"Oh," Faye breathed, enthralled by his expression. "That's . . . uh . . . wonderful!"

He released a low groan and drew her against him, his lips slanting down possessively over hers, his hands roving over her back to press her closer into his warmth. He released her mouth and slung his arms over her shoulders while he gazed intently into her eyes. "I'm not going to forget, Faye. As a matter of fact, as soon as we're out of this mess, I will make darn sure neither of us do."

"I don't know if we'll have the chance." Faye sighed regretfully. "After all, we only have a short time together."

"Really?" He lifted one eyebrow. "Exactly how long is this 'short time'?"

"I'm not sure." Faye wrinkled her nose as she considered it. "We were brought together to defeat the Alchemist. After that, our time together will end."

His eyes assumed a half-believing, half-teasing expression. "What happens if we don't defeat him?"

"He destroys the world, and us along with it."

"We'd better not let that happen, then." He gave her a brief, hard kiss, swooped her up and set her on the mare. "If you're expecting me to disappear in a puff of smoke, though, you're in for a big disappointment."

Faye watched him vault onto the prancing gelding. "I'm not expecting you to disappear at all."

"Really?" He lifted one eyebrow in mock apprehension. "What dastardly thing am I supposed to do instead?"

"You don't do anything," Faye insisted. She took a long breath of cool morning air. "An Ayaldwode and a Wizard are brought together for a mission. When that mission is over, the Ayaldwode is the one who disappears."

OH, GET OUT OF MY HEAD! Kent thought with some ag-
gravation. He winced at the resulting burst of irrita-
tion from Avril, but made no attempt to pretend a
remorse he didn't feel. There wasn't much point—lying this way was impossible, and he was definitely not
sorry for his annoyance. Avril was far too concerned
about his emotional state.

He turned his attention to the woman and horse in
front of him. Faye was wearing the same outfit that
she'd changed into yesterday—rusty brown pants,
green-and-beige shirt, and a forest green jacket. If she
slipped into the woods surrounding them, she could
indeed disappear. He gave his head a quick side-to-side
shake. That was ridiculous. People didn't go around
disappearing, not even someone like Faye. That was a
myth, just like the myths about Wizards, and Ayaldwodes, and Alchemists and missions.

So, why was he starting to believe them? Kent
watched Faye duck to avoid a tree branch, almost forgetting to do so himself. She was so graceful, her body
swayed so naturally on the horse, and she looked so
much at home out here that she could indeed be a wood
sprite. And, unfortunately, he had all the qualifications for Wizardhood. As much as he hated to admit it,
she'd even been accurate this morning. He'd had a
number of casual encounters with women, and he
couldn't put a face to one of them. As a matter of fact,
he could hardly recall his ex-wife's features, either. Not
surprising—he'd made a concerted effort to forget that
whole mess. The familiar cloud of guilt and remorse

settled over him, and he shoved it away. "You don't beat yourself up about the past," Dan had advised. "You learn from it, and put it aside."

Kent had learned from it. He'd learned that "forever" was a concept that was completely beyond him. That might make him something of a jerk, but it certainly didn't mean he was a Wizard.

Faye's horse stopped abruptly, catching both Kent and his mount totally by surprise. The gelding veered to the left to avoid a collision, and Kent almost slipped off. He instinctively tightened his thighs around the animal and watched Faye look up into the sky. She turned two wide, worried eyes toward him. "The helicopter!"

"Get down!" Kent ordered. He leapt to the ground before Kalli had come to a halt, and streaked toward Faye, concerned that she would panic and reveal their presence.

She slid gracefully off her horse, her head still cocked to listen. Although the pulse on her neck fluttered furiously, she didn't appear to be panicking. "They can't see us in here, can they?" she whispered.

"Nope," he said in a normal tone. "And they can't hear us, either." He drew her down to sit under a canopy of trees. "Come to think of it, I can't hear them."

"Listen," she told him.

He did. Moments later, he heard the faint whop-whop, and squeezed an arm around her shoulder. "Just sit still," he warned.

"What about the horses?"

The animals had wandered slightly away from them, and were eagerly munching at the ground. Kent tried to picture how the scene would look from above. "They shouldn't be able to see them, either," he concluded. "Even if they can, a couple of horses wandering around won't tell them anything." He listened to the rushing sounds of the flowing water. "How close are we to the river crossing?"

Faye pressed her ear against his chest. "Not far."

"Do the trees grow right up to the riverbank?"

"Yes."

"And on the other side?"

She thought about it for a moment, then shook her silver-blond head. "Not quite. There's about a hundred meters before the forest begins again." She trembled as the helicopter noises grew louder.

"It's okay," Kent soothed. He caressed her jacketed arm, then impulsively nuzzled his fingers underneath, across the smooth flesh of her abdomen. She released a small, purring moan of pleasure and he felt the tension leave her body. Well, well, he thought with supreme satisfaction. That was one way to keep her from panicking. His own body gave a kick start of recognition, and he held in a sigh. The trouble with this method was that it distracted him, as well.

And why shouldn't it? He had perfect recall of the night before! As a matter of fact, he was tempted to ignore the danger above them, push her sweet, soft body into the leaves, and make darn sure she remembered it, too!

He leaned back to rest his head against a tree trunk. The foliage was so dense here that only a few dappled splashes of sun managed to get through. There was no way those helicopter idiots could see them, and he was confident they would soon go away. And when they did, he'd take Faye across the river, and into cover again, just in case. Then they'd make it to the neighbor's house, and get some help. He desperately wanted to be out of here, and back into the familiarity of civilization, where Faye's fairy tales would no longer seem so believable.

The helicopter was almost directly above them now. As Faye stiffened beside him, he inched his thumb up to touch her breast and she moaned deliciously. Kent clenched his teeth at his own rush of desire. He'd told her the truth this morning—that there was no way he'd forget her as he had others. Those depths of passion, her flowing, liquid response, and the sense of contentment afterward were etched in his memory. Right now, he wanted nothing more than to be with her, to listen to her strange views of the world, to mold her body with his, to watch her eat and sleep and do all the normal things that she somehow made so enchanting.

But it would end. Like she said, they had only a short time together. That idea caused an unexpected sense of bereavement. *Get a grip, MacIntyre,* he ordered himself. He was just uncomfortable with her suggestions that they were heading toward a conclusion he couldn't control. She was wrong about that, just as she was wrong about him being a Wizard. No one was going to disappear. They'd take care of Collingswood, then spend a week or so someplace very private. He relaxed back as he made that decision. After a couple of weeks, he'd be over this infatuation, and she probably would, as well. Their affair would end as his others had, with a touch of regret and a whole lot of relief.

But first, they had to get out of this mess. He listened to the helicopter sounds receding, removed his hand from Faye's warm breast, and straightened. "Listen, babe, as soon as that helicopter is gone, I want you to get across the river and into the trees as fast as you can. Don't wait for me."

She lifted her lashes and looked at him with heavy-lidded, luminous eyes. "What?"

"I want you to get across the river. If that chopper comes back, I'll—"

"But we have to cross together," she said blankly.

"Yes, but you go first and—"

"No, Kent." She pulled away from him, her brow wrinkling along with her nose. "We have to be on the same horse."

Kent sensed another Ayaldwode fable was imminent. "Is this something to do with Wizards?"

"Yes."

"Can't we forget that stuff? I want you to—"

"We can't forget it!" she insisted with some alarm. "It's water, Kent. *Running* water."

Kent listened to the sounds of the river and nodded. "You're right on that count, but . . ."

She heaved a huge, impatient sigh. "Wizards don't like water. They can't control it."

Kent lowered his head and rubbed the prickle on the back of his neck. He really wished she'd stop doing this.

"You can't, can you?" Faye demanded.

"No," he admitted. "My telekinesis doesn't work on water. But so what? I don't want to move it, I just want to ride a horse through it."

Faye clasped his hand between her two palms. "It's *running* water. It will drain your strength if you cross it alone."

At last! A Wizard characteristic he didn't share! "No, it won't," he said gently.

"Yes, it will, Kent! You should know this! You must have crossed running water before!"

"Of course."

"And didn't you get sick?"

The prickles returned to his neck in full force. "I get motion sickness on boats," he growled. "I won't on a horse!"

"You will!" she assured him. "It's a problem all Wizards share. You will sicken when you cross water, unless you're with an Ayaldwode."

"Oh, for Pete's sake, Faye, why should that make any difference?"

Her cheeks were stained red with annoyance. "Because one way or another, all Ayaldwodes are part water nymph."

"Isn't that handy?" Kent rolled his tongue around his cheek. "Do you take turns popping out of the river to hand out motion-sickness potions?"

"No," Faye said very seriously. "We take turns knocking impudent Wizards into the river and seeing if they float." She batted her lashes at him, and he wasn't quite sure if she was serious.

"I can swim," he reminded them both.

"That won't help if a water nymph gets cross with you!"

"Oh." He inched closer and pressed his lips against her temple. "How about if they like you? Huh?"

Her slight body gave a small, delicious shiver. "Then you can't drown," she breathed. She raised her lashes, showing two mischievous eyes. "But you can get awful wet."

"In that case, I'll stop annoying you." He took a slow, sweet kiss from her, then pulled them both to a stand and helped her onto the mare. She patted the space behind her bottom. "Come on. We can both ride Katlin across."

Kent hesitated for a moment, uncertain of his next move. He couldn't actually recall ever riding a horse over a river, but he was pretty certain it wasn't going to make him turn green and throw up, which is what happened every time he got near a boat. If he really wanted to put a stop to this Wizard business, he could get on Kalli and ride alone. He wouldn't get sick, she'd be convinced, and . . .

And he didn't know if he wanted to do that. From macadamia nuts to magical lovemaking, he had all the qualifications for Wizardhood. He might get a little testy about it, but he'd become accustomed to being her Wizard. Proving he wasn't would serve no useful purpose to her, and, if by some remote fluke he did get sick, he'd have one more chunk of evidence that her little fairy tale was true.

He looked up into her adorable, expectant face, and vaulted onto the mare, smiling as he fitted his body behind hers.

He could masquerade as a Wizard a little while longer.

9

FAYE CAREFULLY PARTED the branches and peeked past them into the Taggert yard. There was a fifty-year-old, two-story house, painted red and white, a bright red barn off to one side, a garage at the back the same color, and numerous small buildings behind that. A graveled drive circled in from the roadway. Two vehicles were parked there: the Taggerts' yellow truck, and a dark green station wagon.

Faye and Kent had left the horses about half a mile behind, and covered the remaining distance on foot. There had been no further sign of the helicopter, and there was no sign of anyone at Taggert's place, except for Bill Taggert. The rugged-faced older man was out in the yard, working on his tractor in front of the machine shed, his only company a black Lab. "That's Mr. Taggert," she whispered to Kent.

"And that looks like Mr. Taggert's dog," he whispered back. "He's coming to say hello."

Sure enough, the dog wandered over to sniff at their bush. Faye crooned a reassurance, and the dog left without a bark.

"How did you do that?" Kent hissed.

"Sheeba and I are old friends," Faye explained. "Well, what are we going to do?"

Kent scratched his chin. "I'm not walking up to Mr. Taggert and asking him if I can use his phone. That sounds too darn dangerous for all of us. Besides, I'm not certain his phone is such a good idea. It's probably tapped."

"Oh." Faye rubbed her arms, trying to warm them, to dispel the sudden feeling of panic. "What will we do, then?"

Kent's fingers traced the line of his jaw. "If Taggert needed a part for his tractor, where would he go?"

Faye shrugged. "Into town, I imagine."

"All right. Let's do that, then."

"Do what?"

"Break his tractor, and convince him he should drive into town. If we're lucky, we can hitch a ride without him even knowing it."

Faye gave him a brilliant smile. "You are a terrific Wizard, Kent."

He ruffled her hair and grinned, but made no effort to correct her.

Less than twenty minutes later, they were bumping along in the back of Taggert's old yellow Dodge pickup, hiding underneath a tarp along with a toolbox, bits of hay and straw, and some earthy smells. Sitting guard for them, on the edge of the tarp, was Sheeba.

The truck slowed to a stop and Faye stiffened. "Why are we stopping?" she hissed. "We can't be in town yet. What's happening?"

"How should I know?" Kent whispered back. "I'm in here with you, remember?" He rubbed a thumb along the jumping pulse in her wrist, and she relaxed. Kent's plan had worked perfectly so far. He'd used his telekinetic ability to break a part on the tractor, and then stared at Bill Taggert with total concentration until the older man found the problem. Kent hadn't explained to her how he'd done that, and she hadn't asked. When Taggert stomped into the house to tell his wife he was going to town to get a part, Faye and Kent had slipped into the back of the pickup.

The truck was at a dead stop now, and Faye could hear footsteps on the gravel road, followed by Taggert's gruff voice. "What's going on?"

"FBI," said a male voice.

"FBI?" Taggert repeated. "What're you folks doing way out here?"

There was a rustle of paper. "Have you seen this man?"

"Nope. Who is he?"

"Name's Kent MacIntyre. He's wanted in Denver for assault and robbery. He was sighted in this area yesterday."

Faye began a gasp that was terminated by Kent's hand over her mouth. She swallowed hard, trying to control her alarm.

"What would he be doing up here?" Taggert asked suspiciously. "None of us got nothing to steal, unless he's a cattle rustler."

"We believe he's abducted a Faye Maxwell."

"Miss Faye?" Taggert's voice was pure disbelief. "Naw. Can't be with her. Couldn't get to her place if she didn't want him to. And little Miss Faye, well, she don't hang around with robbers."

"That's our information." The man sounded a bit annoyed. Faye smiled to herself. The people of Neverdale were her friends. The Alchemist should know that. "You alone in there?" the man demanded.

"Yep. All alone."

"Where are you going?"

"Town," Taggert grunted.

"Why?"

"Need som'in."

There was a long, impatient hiss. "I'd like to check the back of your truck."

"Go ahead."

Footsteps sounded around the side of the pickup. Faye felt Kent's shoulders tense, and gave her head a slight shake. "Sheeba," she mouthed to Kent. "Don't worry." Sure enough, the dog growled a warning.

"Can you call off your dog here?" the man shouted.

"Well, now," Taggert drawled. "Old Sheeba, there, she just don't like strangers. Ain't much I can do about it. Kinda agree with her about that, myself."

Sheeba's warning growl turned into a full-fledged fit of barking.

"Seems to me if she don't like strangers, she wouldn't sit in the back of my truck with one," Taggert declared.

"All right!" A foot stomped childishly. "Go on, then. If you see anything, let us know right away. We wouldn't want anything to happen to you. After all, this Kent MacIntyre's a dangerous character."

"So's m'dog," Taggert grunted, his voice sounding rather amused. The pickup started down the road again.

Kent hugged Faye tightly against him. "How did you get that dog to bark?" he whispered in her ear.

"I told you, Sheeba and I are friends," she whispered back. "What are we going to do?"

"If we're lucky, Taggert will park someplace private, and we'll get a chance to sneak out of here."

"And if we're not lucky?"

Kent grinned. "Have your sleeping powder ready, honey, and hope my magnetic field has been fully restored!"

It was the fastest trip to town Faye had taken in a long time. Her own truck was very old, and didn't go at any great speed. *Mr. Taggert must be in a hurry to get that tractor part,* she thought. She'd reimburse him for it, and take him over some of that rhubarb jam he liked so much.

The pickup slowed to enter town, and then stopped, but the engine didn't turn off, and there was no sound of a door opening. Instead, the horn beeped a couple of times, there was a short wait, then someone approached the truck. "How do, Bill," grunted a voice. "Whaddaya want?"

"That's Mr. Norton," Faye whispered to Kent. "He owns the garage in Neverdale."

"Like to bring the truck inside," said Taggert.

"You're going to let *me* work on your truck?" Mr. Norton sounded as if he couldn't believe his ears. "Well, this day should be marked down in history. First the FBI, then Bill Taggert's gonna let me look at his truck!"

"FBI's been here?" Taggert drawled thoughtfully. "What for?"

"Claim some yahoo abducted little Miss Faye. Kinda hard to believe, but ..."

"They stopped me on the road," said Taggert. "Wanted to check my truck, but old Sheeba back there wasn't having none of it."

"That so?" There was a pregnant pause. "Well, you just pull right on in, Bill. I'll be closin' the door behind you. Bet you don't want anyone else to know you had me look at your truck."

"Oh, damn," Kent muttered.

"It's all right," Faye whispered back. "These people are my friends."

The pickup slid into the garage, there was the sound of an overhead door closing, then the engine switched off. Taggert got out of the vehicle, Kent stiffened, and Faye patted his hand. "It's okay," she whispered again in his ear. There was silence, the murmur of men's voices.

A number of footsteps returned to the truck. "It's okay," Faye called. "It's just me." She ignored Kent's hissed breath, and pushed aside the tarp to pat Sheeba's head. "Thank you," she murmured gratefully.

"Well, Miss Faye," Taggert drawled. "I kinda thought you were in there when Sheeba put up such a fuss. You all right?"

"I'm fine." Faye stood and brushed the dust off her slacks. Beside her, Kent was slowly getting to his feet, his dark eyes flashing his concern.

"Who's that with you?" Taggert demanded.

"Oh, this is Kent MacIntyre." Faye motioned around the group, consisting of Mr. Taggert, a sandy-haired, angular man of about thirty, and a short man of about the same age, with his arm around the shoulders of a plump, red-haired woman. The sandy-haired man had an old shotgun of some sort that he was pointing straight at Kent's head. Beside the woman were two redheaded children, staring with wide blue eyes from Faye to Kent and back again.

Faye performed the introductions. "Kent, this is Mr. Taggert, and Mr. and Mrs. Norton, and their children, Sandra and Timmy. Oh, and the man with the rifle is Matt Jamison."

Kent nodded silently at the group.

Taggert took a step toward them. "You this MacIntyre fellow those phony-baloney FBI goons are looking for?"

"That's right." Kent held both of his hands in front of his chest. "I'm not armed, sir, and I am really not all that dangerous. However, those men—"

"Sure as hell don't work for the FBI," Taggert interrupted. "Who are they?"

"They're after me," Faye explained. "I hope you don't mind us getting a ride with you. We had to get into town and we didn't want to involve you in this."

"Pleased to help you out," Taggert said, nodding. His eyes squinted into a frown as he studied her. "What happened to your face?"

Faye's fingers went to the bruise on her right cheek. "Some men came to my house. They had a helicopter and they wanted me to give them something." She slid an arm around Kent and grabbed a handful of shirt. "Kent stopped them."

"Did he, now? And how did he do that?"

Faye looked up at Kent. His clothes were covered with dust, he could definitely use a shave, and she thought he looked capable of handling a million of Collingswood's men. "Why, he's a Wizard, Mr. Taggert," she exclaimed. "He can do anything."

"WHEN I GOT THERE, they were dragging her toward the helicopter and I managed to stop them," Kent concluded. "We headed over to Taggert's place and snuck a ride here."

The tall sandy-haired man named Matt crossed his arms over his checkered shirt. "Where'd you two spend the night?"

"In the woods," Kent said easily.

Matt gave Kent a look of stern disapproval, and Kent grinned at him. They were in the corner of Hank Norton's garage, right in front of the workbench, which was filled with a random assortment of parts in various states of disrepair. On the wall hung about fifty old calendars, all featuring well-developed women with nothing covering their assets. Kent was leaning against a wall, surrounded by a semicircle of men: Bill Taggert, Hank Norton and Matt Jamison. Faye was in a back room with the two children and their mother. She hadn't wanted to leave Kent, but the youngsters had begged so sweetly for one of her stories that she'd finally given in, after he—and the other men—had assured her he was in no danger.

So far, Kent didn't appear to be. He'd told the men the bare bones of the story—a group of thugs had flown up to Faye's place and attacked her, requesting secret information that had belonged to her father. Kent wasn't sure how much of it they believed, and he didn't much care. Right now, all he wanted was to get to a phone and talk to Dan.

Matt looked up and down Kent's narrow frame with frank disbelief. "How'd you get her away from four armed men?"

"They weren't that smart," Kent growled. "Listen, I don't want to involve you people. I just need to use a phone. There must be police . . ."

Matt thrust his tongue into his cheek. "There's police somewhere. Highway patrol, too—but there's no one in town right now. As for the phone, well, they're all down."

"Really?" Kent drawled. "All of them?" He flicked his gaze around the group, assessing the probability that this was the truth.

"That's right," Norton said, nodding. "They've been down since last night. It happens sometimes, usually in winter, when we get a blizzard."

From the open door of the back room, Kent could hear Faye's voice, spinning a tale to the children. "And then, four evil men came down from the sky, and captured the princess . . ." Kent felt something squeeze painfully in his chest at the sound. He gave himself a mental shake. "So there're no phones in Neverdale, eh?"

"Don't look like it," Bill Taggert drawled. "Somethin' seems to have happened to the main line." He winked at Kent. "Maybe the FBI had somethin' to do with it."

"Maybe." It was a possibility.

"Town's full of those FBI folks, too," Norton went on. "They've been everywhere, asking everyone about Faye and about you." He hooked his thumbs into the belt sagging below the bulge of his belly. "Now, Faye there, well, she's a special little lady, all right. None of us want to see anything happenin' to her. That right, boys?"

"Right enough," Taggert agreed. "Why, I never forgot the way old Glen helped me with my well. As for you, Hank, no one would have found that little boy of yours when he wandered off. He'd have died if Faye there hadn't found him for you."

Hank nodded at Kent. "If Faye says you're who you say you are, well, that's good enough for me." A car pulled up in front of Hank's pumps, heralded by the ringing of the inside bell. Hank swore. "I'll be right back," he called over his shoulder as he headed out to the front. "Don't do nothin' without me."

"We're not going to do anything, period!" Matt announced. He turned to Taggert. "Those men told you this character here was a criminal. Right?"

"That's true," Taggert replied. "But—"

"And they were hiding in the back of your truck," Matt continued. He looked accusingly at Kent. "We don't know this man. This . . . MacIntyre, here, has obviously taken advantage of Faye." He leered. "In more ways than one."

Kent lunged out from the wall, and Taggert put a hand in front of his chest. "Calm down, now. Matt don't mean nothing. He's just got aspirations towards Miss Faye himself. Ain't that so, Matt?"

Matt scowled. "I just don't think we should help a criminal. Faye can hide out at Hank's place until—"

"Forget it!" Kent shook his head. "The lady stays with me, and I'm not hanging around, thanks."

"Why not?" Matt demanded. "If you're who you say you are, you should want to wait for the police."

"For how long?" Kent retorted. "You said the place was filled with those men. We'd be lucky to stay out of sight for two hours, much less the twenty-four it'll probably take for the phones to get repaired."

There was dead silence. The clock on the wall ticked with unnecessary loudness. From the other room, came the soft trill of Faye's voice. No one said a word. Kent shifted from one foot to the other, wondering if Norton was now telling another neighbor about his unexpected guests. Faye's voice stopped, a child screamed, then the redheaded boy dashed from the back room. "Daddy!" he hollered. "Sandra hit me."

Taggert reached out an arm, and missed both kids. The woman ran past after the children, and the front door slammed. "You haven't seen any strangers in town?" asked a man's voice.

"Ain't seen no one," Norton drawled. "That'll be twelve dollars even. Hey, Timmy, stop that."

"But Sandra hit me," the youngster's voice whined.

The woman disappeared from view into the front. "Come on, you two. You come with me."

"But Sandra hit me," the child wailed. "I missed the end of Faye's story."

"Well, he bit me!" Sandra countered. "I missed the end too. Look at my arm, Dad."

Kent winced, hoping desperately that the man wouldn't pick up on the child's revelation. For a second, he thought it might be all right. Then came Norton's voice—"Get your hand off my boy!"—followed by a woman's scream.

"Is there a back door?" Kent mouthed.

Taggert gestured toward the dark hall to their right leading past the storage room. "Down there," he muttered under his breath. Kent took a couple of running steps, then stopped and turned. Taggert and Matt were striding toward the front. Matt was carrying his shotgun.

Kent sighed and shook his head. He couldn't leave these people to take the heat for him. He dashed past them, heard a scream from outside, and took a brief, careful peek out the scratched glass of the overhead door.

It was a good trick. He really had to admire it, even though he was certain it was going to be the death of him. The two bogus FBI men weren't bothering with guns anymore. Oh, one of them had one in his hand, aimed at Norton and his wife. In his other hand, he was clutching the wrist of the little boy.

The second man was the one with the brains. He had an even better weapon—the gasoline hose. He was calmly and methodically spraying the ground with it, letting gas splash onto the building.

"Kent?" Faye whispered. She'd come up to stand beside him, and was now staring out the window. "Oh, no!" she exclaimed. She clutched his arm. "Matt. He—"

"Oh, great!" Kent said, groaning as Matt leapt out the front door, clutching the shotgun. Kent pictured the shotgun on the ground, and, just to be safe, had it slide out of anyone's reach. The gunman shouted an order, and Matt obediently put his hands behind his neck and moved to stand with Norton.

"Thank you." Faye sighed with a relief that Kent didn't appreciate.

"Are you . . . involved with that Matt character?" he asked as they watched Taggert move to join the others.

"He sometimes likes to take me places. What should we do now?"

"I don't know." Kent curled his top lip and eyed the sandy-haired Matt. "I don't think Matt is your type, Faye. He's too . . . uh . . . aggressive."

"He's really quite sweet," she whispered. "What is that man doing?"

The fellow with the hose had set it down. He now reached into his inside pocket and pulled out an old flip-top windproof lighter. "MacIntyre!" he shouted as he opened the top and flicked it to life. "You've got ten seconds to get out here with the woman."

"I'm surrendering," Kent whispered to Faye. "You go out the back. You can—"

"An Ayaldwode stays with her Wizard," Faye interrupted. "They're looking for me, Kent. They're going to keep at these people until they get me. I can't let them get hurt."

She was frightened, and she was probably in as much danger as these people, but naturally, her first thoughts were of them. Kent's admiration for her took a tremendous leap upward. "You are one brave lady," he muttered.

"Not really." She thrust out her chin and took his hand. "I'm with a Wizard. As soon as we are away from here, you can use your magic and overpower them."

That shouldn't be any problem. He could stop the car whenever he wanted, and he could surely handle two men. "All right," he agreed. "As soon as we drive away from here, we'll take care of them." He bent to give her a quick kiss, then regretfully pulled back. "Don't blow up anything!" he shouted. "We're coming."

"You come out first, MacIntyre, with your hands on top of your head."

"Yeah, yeah, yeah," Kent mumbled. "I know that." He pushed Faye behind him. "If they start to shoot, don't come out," he whispered. He put his hands in the required position, gritted his teeth and peeked around the door. No one had moved, and the gun was still pointed at Norton's little crowd. Kent took a cautious step outside, then another. Faye crept out behind him.

"Send the woman over here," ordered the man with the lighter. Faye hesitated, he held up the lighter, and she reluctantly wandered over to stand beside the red-haired woman.

The lighter idiot slid his free hand into a pocket. "Take off your jacket," he ordered Kent. "Real slow."

Terrific. All this, and they were going to steal his jacket! Kent sighed resentfully, carefully pulled off his leather jacket and dropped it in the pool of gasoline. At least they'd have to have it cleaned.

"Turn around! Hands on top of your head and don't move an inch."

Kent reluctantly turned his back to Mr. Torch while mentally running through his list of diminishing options. He heard footsteps, then something sharp jabbed into his arm. He glanced over his shoulder, and saw the flickering lick of the flame.

Then it was almost dark, and he was on the ground, and everything was very, very fuzzy.

10

"MISS ALFAYE MERLINE," Collingswood's voice oozed. "I see rumors of your demise were greatly exaggerated!" He pulled the door closed behind him, nodded at his big blond henchman, and strolled into her living room.

Faye resisted the urge to shrink back in her sofa. She had no reason to be frightened of this man now. She wasn't alone. She had her Wizard with her.

She glanced to her right. Kent was slumped, sideways, beside her. His hands were handcuffed in front of him, although, right now, that precaution didn't appear necessary. His head lolled down so his chin touched his chest, his eyes were only partly open, and his demeanor was that of total exhaustion.

She wasn't quite sure what was wrong with him. He'd been like this ever since he'd collapsed at Norton's garage, and had remained in this stupor throughout the helicopter ride back to her cottage. She hadn't seen anyone do anything to him, and, although she was very frightened, she had every confidence that, sooner or later, her Wizard would regain his strength and defeat the Alchemist once and for all. She just wished he'd hurry up and get on with it.

Collingswood sat down in her green chair and folded his hands in his lap. He raised his voice slightly. "Mr. MacIntyre. How are you feeling?"

Kent's head came up a couple of inches, then fell back down.

"Perfect," Collingswood said, nodding. He looked over at Faye. "There's no point in looking to MacIntyre for help. As you can see, there's not much he can do."

Faye lifted her chin. "He—he's just tired. When he wakes up..."

"He's not going to wake up, Alfaye—at least, not the way you mean. We've given him D4515-12B. Do you know what that is?"

Faye shook her head, as slow, cold tendrils of fear started at her toes and began creeping upward. He couldn't defeat Kent, she assured herself. He couldn't.

"It's actually a formula we were working on to slow the aging process of the skin. Unfortunately, it had a terrible side effect, and had to be shelved."

"Wh-what side effect?" Faye asked apprehensively.

"It slows all your bodily functions, causing debilitating exhaustion." He lifted an eyebrow. "It's pretty much a permanent effect, I'm afraid."

"Wh-why...?"

"You know why. I don't know how MacIntyre does what he does, but I do know these men I've hired aren't at all eager to tangle with him. After I heard their stories, I realized I would either have to have him shot, or drug him. I needed him alive, so I chose the latter." He nodded with satisfaction. "It appears that I chose right."

Faye looked over at Kent. He made a monumental effort, lifted his head and blinked open two unfocused dark eyes before his head fell again.

"He can hear us," Collingswood told her. "He feels things. He knows what's going on. He just can't do anything about it." His pale green eyes blinked myopically around the room, then focused in on her. "Now, Alfaye, I have a few questions I want answered, and then we'll talk...."

"Y-you're wasting your time," Faye said desperately. "My father is dead now, and I—"

"I know about Glendon's death," he interrupted. "Heart attack, wasn't it?" He lifted an eyebrow at her. "It took a little time, but the people I've hired are fairly efficient. They never would have found this place without following MacIntyre. You and Glendon did a good job hiding yourselves. I really thought you were dead, until you showed up at my labs."

Faye shuddered back into the cushions.

"Don't look like that!" he ordered. "I'm not a sadist. I don't enjoy hurting people. I just want the Mozelle formula. You give it to me, and ..."

"I don't know—"

"You know it, all right!" he interjected. "You worked with Glendon developing it. You broke into my labs and destroyed my experiments, changed every record. You couldn't have done that if you didn't know it."

"I won't tell you," Faye whispered. "I won't. I know what you'll do to me, but . . ."

"Your father said that, too," Collingswood purred. "I changed his mind, and I'll change yours. Don't let it come to that." He took a pen and paper out of his jacket pocket and held them toward her. "Write out the formula. Now. I'm not going to be as naive as I was last time. I'm going to keep you here while I test it. I can have everything I need here in a few hours, and you seem to have a cute little laboratory in the back of that greenhouse of yours. As long as you cooperate, there'll be no need for any . . . unpleasant persuasion."

"L-leave h-h-her-r-r-r a-al-lone," Kent stuttered.

Collingswood took no notice of him. "Well?" he prompted. "I'm waiting."

"You don't want to know the Mozelle formula," Faye said desperately. "It's evil. It's—"

"It's also a fabulous weapon that can make me very, very wealthy." His pale eyes glinted impatiently. "I have to have it, Alfaye. I've spent a great deal of money on my own research, and on finding you. My backer is getting impatient for results." He shook the paper in his hand. "Write out the formula."

Faye pressed herself against Kent's arm. His body was cooler than normal, but his touch gave her strength. She tossed back her head. "No. I'm afraid you aren't wise enough to possess Mozelle, Joseph."

Collingswood's thin lips turned down in a fearsome scowl. "How are your legs, Alfaye?"

"M-my legs?" Faye repeated. She put a hand down, touching the scars through the fabric.

"I didn't like doing that to you," Collingswood oozed. "But it was the only way to get Glendon to talk."

Kent muttered an obscenity, tried to stand, and sank back down.

"Perhaps you do need some persuasion." Collingswood glanced over at the burly blond. "My briefcase, please."

The blond handed it over. The room fell silent as the Alchemist clicked open the black case. Faye looked from him, to Kent, to the big blond man. She felt suddenly felt very cold, and almost paralyzed with terror. Something horrible was going to happen, and it was going to happen right now.

Collingswood took a glass vial out of his briefcase, and held it up. Faye's heart stopped beating. "You know what this is, don't you, Alfaye?"

She squeezed her eyes shut, remembering the room, and her father, tied to a chair, watching while Collingswood dropped this substance onto her. "The formula!" Collingswood demanded.

Faye shook her head.

Collingswood slowly got to his feet, and started toward them.

FROM THE WAY THE MEN acted, Faye could tell they had no idea they were dealing with a Wizard.

They had made some concessions, she admitted as the big blond man unlocked the door to her garden shed. Even though it was very dark, she could see that her rakes, hoes, and shovels had been thrown on the ground outside in an untidy heap. They had also removed all her flowerpots, and her wheelbarrow. However, there were no guards stationed at the door, and the blond didn't bother pulling out a gun before shoving her unceremoniously inside.

After her eyes adjusted to the thick darkness, she could see why. Kent was certainly in no condition to do anything. He remained, as the Alchemist had predicted, in a slumped heap beside the wooden shelving unit, his left hand handcuffed to one of the supports. "Oh, Kent," she whispered.

She darted over to kneel in front of him. His eyes were closed, and the pulse under her searching fingers was light and slow. His body was almost as cold as the concrete pad under her knees. Faye wrapped her arms around him. "Oh, Kent," she said again.

He grunted something, but didn't move.

Faye leaned back on her heels and listened. There was the faint sound of the door to her house closing, then no noise at all, except the wind, howling ominously around the shed. "I know," Faye murmured. "We don't have much time."

She returned her attention to the limp man in her arms. This was not going to be at all easy. She had no idea how to go about doing it, but it was her last, desperate hope, and she was going to give it her best shot. She pressed her lips against his, but they were cold and unresponsive, and his body gave no sign of movement. Faye felt a tingle of alarm, and pushed it away. This simply had to work. She kissed him again, smoothing her hand down his cheek. "Oh, Kent," she breathed for a third time.

His eyelids fluttered slightly and he released a muttered moan. "F-Faye?"

"Yes!" she exclaimed. "Yes, yes, it's me." She kissed him again, caressing his face, his lips, his temple, and smoothing a hand down his shirted chest.

His eyelids flickered again. "Faye?" His tongue came out to touch his lips. "Okay?"

"Yes, yes, I'm okay," she assured him eagerly. "But we have a big problem, Kent. Joseph has the Mozelle formula." She took a breath. "I had to tell him. I had to. I know I shouldn't have, but...I...I couldn't think of anything else to do."

"Not your fault," he moaned through barely open lips. "C-Collings . . . he . . ."

"That's right," Faye said sadly. "He was going to do it to you, Kent. He was going to use that acid on you, just like he did to me." She hugged his head against her. "That's what happened to my legs. I know how it feels. I couldn't let him do that to you. I couldn't."

He tried to lift his head, but it lolled back against her chest. "Got away then . . ."

"Well, yes, but Joseph pretty much let us go. He didn't realize my father hadn't told him everything, and he had his men push our car into a river." She shuddered at the memory. "He couldn't have known that anyone loved by a water nymph can't drown."

"Should have told me," Kent mumbled.

"I couldn't tell you." She folded her arms around him, hugging his chilled body to her. "It was my fault last time, Kent. My father told Joseph the first part of Mozelle because of me. I didn't think you'd help me if you knew."

His head rose off of her shoulder, only to fall again. "Not much help."

"Of course you are!" She took his head between her hands, holding it so she could see it. His eyes were open a very tiny bit, but there was no sign of strength. "You're my Wizard," she reminded him.

His lips flicked in a ghost of a smile. "No." His left hand moved slightly, jangling the chain. "Can't do it." His tongue moistened his lips again. "Tried. Can't."

"Of course you can't," Faye said impatiently. "The drug drained your magnetic field. We have to fix it."

"Can't," he said again, and there was deep despair in his groan. "Effects . . . permanent."

"Maybe on others, although I'm not convinced. I know it's not nice to say, but I don't think Joseph is much of a chemist." She moved her lips over his, and this time, she felt a tremble of a response. "We are going to restore your power. We have to do it right now, so we'll have to be quiet." She slowly lowered him to the concrete floor. His head lolled to one side, then gradually straightened. She slid her hands under his brown cotton shirt.

His forehead furrowed. "What . . . ?"

"We have to make love." The sensation of his flesh under hers caused a slow, expectant tingle of reaction. "We have to, Kent. Together, a Wizard and an Ayald-wode are magic. My mother told me that. I think it means that we can restore your power this way."

Kent moaned—a hard, harsh sound of despair. "Can't do that."

Faye hadn't considered that possibility. "You have to," she said desperately. "You have to. Joseph is plan-ning on doing something terrible. He's going to test Mozelle in Miller's pond." She bent to kiss him. "As soon as it's dawn, Mozelle with be activated by the sun's rays. There will be terrible destruction, Kent. Terri-ble."

He raised his free arm about six inches off the ground before it fell. "Faye . . ."

"He's taking me with him," Faye went on urgently. "He's taking me with him, and I think he's going to leave me there."

"No . . ."

"He plans on making it look as if I did it," Faye whis-pered. "He's going to make it look as if I was doing one of my father's experiments on the pond." The horror of it settled around her, and she fought it. "We have to stop him, Kent. I know we can, as long as I can fix your magnetic field." She pulled her hand out from under his shirt, and fumbled with the clasp on his jeans. "We have to make love," she panted. "We have to. . . ."

His arm lifted off the ground, his cold fingers closing around her wrist. Faye gasped a startled breath of desperation, and looked into his dark, almost-closed eyes. "W-won't work," he slurred. "No Wizard, Faye."

"I don't care," she cried. She threw herself onto his limp form, almost sobbing. "I don't care if you're a Wizard or not. I need you now. I need you. Please . . ."

His hand was on her back now, still cold, but at least there. "I'll . . . try," he grunted.

That was all Faye needed to hear. She squirmed on top of him, pressing hard, frantic kisses on his lips, encouraged by a faint tremor of response. Then she was kneeling beside him, struggling to remove her slacks, pushing up his shirt, tearing a fingernail as she unzipped his jeans. Her fingers slid impatiently inside to close around him, anticipating the hard, throbbing, masculine flesh she remembered feeling before.

It wasn't going to be that simple, she discovered. He might have been right. This just might not be possible. No! She had to make this happen. She sucked in air, wishing she'd had more experience than their one evening together. Kent had taken charge then, but he was in no condition to do so now. *Think*, she ordered her panicking brain. *Think*. She'd been asleep. He had woken her. How had he done that?

She stretched out on his partly-clothed figure, stroking her body against his, and kissed him again. There was definitely a response this time. "We can do this," she murmured. "I can do this." She began squirming down him, unbuttoning his shirt, pressing tentative kisses against his skin. He groaned—a deep, guttural sound of encouragement. She kept going, down his abdomen, down to the unfamiliar sensation of hair, loving his feel, his taste, his scent. Then she was pushing aside his legs, fastening her lips around his now hardening shaft. His body gave a slow, long shudder, and his hand came up to her neck. "Faye!"

Suddenly his need seemed to match her own. He pulled her down to him, his lips closing around a breast while his hand caressed her back with growing urgency. He spoke her name again, as his fingers found the slick sheath between her legs, and his thumb curled into the mat of hair surrounding it, stroking her with impatient desire. Then he was guiding her onto him, and she heard her own voice, purring her pleasure as she felt them join, as she felt him thrust deeper and deeper into her, folding her down to him, holding her as close, as tightly as he could, his lips, his body possessing hers. She sobbed agreement into his ear, moving urgently and instinctively with his rhythm. There was no time for coherent thought; there was just the hot comfort of his maleness, and a flashing regret that she might never experience this again. "Oh, darling," he cried. "Faye!"

He arched sharply under her. There was a tremendous burst of energy, and she contracted with a million sparkles of sensation, collapsing upon him while he groaned in his own ecstasy.

Faye lay there for a few minutes, listening as his raspy breathing evened out. Then, very slowly, she lifted her head.

He appeared to be asleep. His eyes were closed, his lips curled into a small, contented smile. "Kent?" she whispered.

He didn't move.

Faye carefully detached herself from him, and slowly replaced her clothing. This could very well have restored his power, she assured herself. It just might take a little time to work. Even if it didn't, *she* felt better now, better able to deal with what she might face.

The wind howled outside the shed. Faye quickly rearranged Kent's clothes, then cuddled down onto him. "You are a Wizard," she told him. "You are my Wizard, and you were definitely worth waiting for." She lay her head on his chest, realizing she'd done exactly what her mother had warned her not to do. "I love you," she whispered into Kent's ear. She pressed a final kiss to his lips, and his eyes flashed open, then closed.

A key scraped in the lock, and the door opened. "Come, Alfaye," purred Joseph Collingswood. "It's time to see if this formula of yours really works."

A HELICOPTER WAS close by. The sound of it slipped into Kent's consciousness, tangling with the desperate blasts of concern Avril was transmitting. *Cut it out!* he ordered. *I'm fine!*

He opened his eyes, and discovered that his surroundings disagreed. Apparently he wasn't all that fine. He was in a shed of some sort, and it was very dark and very cold. Someone must want to keep him here, because his left wrist was handcuffed to a set of wooden shelves. He ordered them undone, but they completely ignored him. *What the hell?*

Memory returned to him in swift, painful flashes. The drug! Collingswood! Faye! Oh, Lord, they had Faye!

Everything else came back to him, as well. His complete helplessness, her frantic theory on how to restore his power, the hot, desperate passion of being with her. He dropped his head into his free hand, groaning aloud as he realized the circumstances. He was still trapped here, still as helpless as before. Faye would be in some panic now. She'd know he wasn't a Wizard. She'd know the situation was totally unsalvageable. Damn!

He took a long breath of cold air, and tried to remember exactly what she'd said. Miller's pond. Collingswood was testing Mozelle at Miller's pond, and he was taking Faye with him! Kent had no idea where Miller's pond was, but even if he did, he couldn't do anything!

He'd contact Avril. She'd do something. She could call somebody. A foggy remembrance slid into his mind. He'd been in touch with her before, through the hazy grogginess of that drug. That's why she was so worried now.

At least Collingswood had been mistaken about the drug. What had Faye said—something about him being a poor chemist? She must have been right. Kent felt much better now, his mind clearer and sharper than it had been since Norton's garage. Perhaps that was due to Faye's presence. He sniffed the air, catching her sunshine scent; sensing, too, the lingering sparkle in the air from their lovemaking. "I love you," she'd whispered. He could still hear those words, and, if she were here, he might just say them back to her. No, that was impossible. A Wizard didn't fall in love. Then again, he wasn't a Wizard, was he? If he was, he wouldn't be in this mess. He gave the manacle on his hand a furious glare. If only this thing was gone . . .

A hard, cold tingle of energy sprang from his body toward his shackle.

Then, as easy as taking a step, as amazing as the first time he'd made it work, as simple as thinking the thought, the metal bracelet around his wrist opened.

MILLER'S POND, Kent thought desperately. *M-I-L-L-E-R . . . Ah, forget it*. It was too hard to transmit something that specific, especially while he was running full speed through this forest.

Fortunately, the forest seemed really anxious for him to make good time. The wind pushed at his back with forceful encouragement, and whipped in front of him to clear leaves and twigs out of his path, almost as if it were as frantic as he was to rescue her.

Frantic was exactly how Kent was feeling. He knew his chances of finding Collingswood at Miller's pond were slim at best—after all, the Alchemist was in a helicopter, and Kent was on foot. However, he could get there before dawn—before Mozelle was activated—and he could get Faye out of the danger zone. He could do that. It would be close, because dawn appeared to be less than an hour away, but he could do it. He *had* to do it.

Kent had expected to find at least one man guarding him, but there hadn't been a soul when he'd left the shed. Then again, in the condition he'd been in, he hadn't been that much of a threat. Still, it was kind of odd.

He pushed his way through the last of the trees, and came to a full, dead stop at the place where Faye's green pickup had been parked.

It was gone.

Of course. Collingswood would have arranged for it to be moved to Miller's pond, if he wanted to implicate Faye. Kent had been half expecting it, but finding his suspicions confirmed was a major disappointment. He gasped in a couple of ragged breaths and headed down the road at a full gallop.

He was just approaching the first sharp turn when he heard the quiet purr of a car engine. He didn't even consider hitchhiking, this would be another of Collingswood's crowd. If it wasn't—too bad. Kent needed a vehicle. Now.

He slid into the bushes beside the road. This car would soon be breaking down—nothing serious, of course; something that could be easily repaired. He ran through a list of possibilities, mumbling them out loud. "Not a tire . . . I don't have time to change it. Distributor cap, maybe. Or a fan belt . . ."

Whoever was driving down the road was doing so without the benefit of headlights; the sound of the car's engine the only indication of its approach. Finally it rounded the curve. The motor sputtered, and the car slid to a stop almost directly across from him. He picked up a rock and crept forward.

The car door opened, and a figure got out—a man, who slammed the door with an abrupt, familiar gesture, leaned his back against it, and swore very loudly. "If that's you, Kent, you'd better be able to fix my car in one hell of a hurry. And if it isn't Kent, you'd better come out of there with your hands up, because I've got a gun the size of New York trained on those bushes."

The rock dropped out of Kent's hand as he slowly rose to his full height. "You don't even own a gun," he called out in a voice that shook slightly. He staggered out of the bushes, unable to believe the sight in front of him.

A craggy-featured, scowling-faced, gray-haired man stood beside a maroon sedan, his arms folded across his chest, his eyes cold and angry. "God damn you, Kent," he snarled as Kent neared. "Where the hell have you been? I have told you and told you that you've got to keep in touch if you're going to do any work for me! That means using the *telephone*, not your *sister!* She's been calling me on my cellular phone every ten minutes, convinced you're about to kick the—"

"Could you yell at me later?" Kent interrupted. "I've got a bit of a problem...." He rested a shoulder against the car, swallowing.

Dan straightened, muscle by muscle. "That bad, is it?"

Kent was silent for a moment. "And then some," he said, and he was totally unable to control the crack in his voice.

11

DAN WRAPPED HIS FISTS tighter around the steering wheel, guiding the car through the dim light of early dawn. "Avril told me to hold off going to Salt Lake City until I heard from you. According to her, it wasn't all that serious. Then, today she calls, screaming and ranting that she's picking up garbage from you and something is terribly wrong and I have to find you for her." He sighed and raised his eyebrows. "Well, you know how she is. I already knew this was big-time shit, so I—"

"Thanks for coming," Kent interrupted. "I am more than happy to see you." He ate a couple of macadamia nuts Dan had provided while peering out the window, comparing their location to the detailed area map resting on his knees.

"I didn't come alone," Dan went on. "Government boys should be down here in a couple of hours."

"What government boys?"

"The ones I notified as soon as I tracked down Collingswood's backer."

Kent checked the map again. "Take the next left. Who's Collingswood's backer?"

"Felix Bristol." Dan shot a knowing look across the car. "You heard of him?"

"No. Can't you go any faster?"

Dan ignored the last part of his statement, probably because Kent had been saying it for the past ten minutes. "Bristol is a weapons broker. Apparently he's given Collingswood plenty of dough to produce this Mozelle stuff." Dan shook his head. "He's a bad one to cross."

"So am I," Kent said savagely. "I'll get Collingswood, but right now, I'm more concerned about Faye."

"The World Environmental Agency folks are pretty keen on talking to her." Dan grunted. He wheeled the car around the turn without bothering to slow down. "They were tickled pink when I told them you'd found her."

"Let's hope she's here to talk to." Kent tugged Dan's jacket tighter around his shoulders. "I sure screwed this up, Dan. Big time."

"You did okay," Dan said brusquely. "A little over-confident, maybe, but that's your nature." He softened his voice. "We'll get her, kid."

"We'd better." Kent pushed a stray hair out of his face. "I'm not sure I can live with myself if we don't." He knew he was speaking the literal truth. "Turn here!"

Dan yanked the car to the right, and they bumped along a narrow, rutted road, down a steep incline, toward a small, misshapen body of water. It was more a slough than a pond, and its stench curled Kent's nostrils, but filled the rest of him with satisfaction. This must be the place.

The now familiar noise of a helicopter confirmed his suspicions. Collingswood and friends must have decided to stick around as long as possible to watch the disaster they had created. The car cleared the trees, and Kent saw two things: Faye's little body kneeling beside the pond in total despair, and some distance to her left, the blue-and-gray chopper, its blades just starting to turn.

"Back rotary blade!" Dan shouted as he wheeled the car toward the water. "Snap it!"

Kent leapt out of the car before it had stopped moving. The rear blade was spinning so fast he couldn't identify it, but he remembered what it looked like, gathered all his energy, and rocketed it forward. The machine began a huge, back-and-forth shuddering, then the engine switched off. Kent took a step toward it, and Dan's large hand clamped to his shoulder. "I'll handle them."

Kent blinked at him. He had known Dan for some years, but had only seen *this* man a few times, and had almost forgotten about him. Easygoing, nondescript Dan had transformed into a dangerously lethal creature, who did indeed own a gun as big as New York and who handled it with an easy familiarity, which suggested he'd done this several million times. "Get the girl into the car," Dan ordered as the helicopter thumped to the ground. "I'll put these characters in the trunk."

Kent didn't even bother to watch.

FAYE KNELT AT THE water's edge, weeping. She knew something was going on behind her, but she wasn't interested. All she could think about was the terrible, terrible things that were going to happen very shortly, and that there was nothing anyone could do to stop it.

She peeked through her fingers at the pond. It was still there—the dusky, moving circles signifying the presence of Mozelle. She had seen them many times before, at first with delight, then, later, when she and her father had realized what they had created, with dawning horror.

That's how she felt now. Total horror, along with the faint comfort that her father was not here to see it. He had given up so much to prevent this from happening, and now, because of her, it was all too real. She had failed to protect his legacy, she had failed to protect her Wizard, and now she was going to have to watch as she failed to protect her world. From around her came the rushing sounds of animals, trying to vacate the area, and a noise on the wind that sounded like her name. But it wasn't the wind calling her. It was . . . No . . . Or . . . ? She felt an arm enclose her, pulling her to her feet. "Faye! Oh, Faye, honey!"

Faye found herself staring into two dark, amber-tinted eyes, while two arms hugged her so tightly her ribs creaked. "Kent?" she asked. She put a wondering hand against his cheek, feeling his face, feeling his warmth seep into her, feeling his exotic scent swirling around them both. "Kent?"

"That's me, babe." He snuggled her into his shoulder, his body trembling against hers. "Oh, Lord," he groaned. "Am I glad to see you!"

It took her a moment to understand. "It worked," she whispered. "Your magnetic field . . ."

"Is fine and well, thanks to you." He gave her one brief kiss, then began urging her toward a vehicle she hadn't noticed before. "Let's get out of here!"

Faye took a couple of steps, then resisted. "It's too late, Kent."

He stopped and scowled down at her. "What do you mean, it's too late? It isn't dawn yet."

"He put it all in," she whispered. She wrapped herself against him again, sobbing into his shoulder. "Oh, Kent, I'm so glad you're here to be with me, and I'm ever so sorry you won't live through this, but he put it all in."

Kent untangled her from him and peered into her face. "What exactly are you telling me, honey?"

"He put the whole vial in," Faye gasped. "I saw him do it, Kent. He poured it in, and I begged him not to, and he did, and . . ."

"Shh. Calm down, now." His hand caressed her back, soothing her as it always had before. "Just tell me. He put all the Mozelle in the vial into the pond. Is that right?"

"Yes, yes. And, oh, Kent, everything is going to die. You, me. The animals, the plants . . ." She buried her head into him. "Neverdale!"

"Neverdale?" Kent repeated. "It will spread to Neverdale?"

"Yes, yes, it will, and . . . beyond. Perhaps . . . perhaps the whole state!"

Kent growled a very unwizardly word, took her hand, and pulled her toward the car. "Come on."

"It's no use," Faye sniffed. "We can't get away. Nothing can get away. The deer . . . the rabbits . . . everything is going to die."

"Yeah, I gathered that." He kept going, practically lifting her off the ground with each impatient step.

Joseph Collingswood and his blond companion were being held at gunpoint by an older, gray-haired man whose craggy features showed an intensity that made her shiver.

Kent glanced down at her. "It's okay, babe. This is my . . . uh . . . counselor, Dan Stuart. Dan, this is Alfaye Merline."

"A pleasure," Dan grunted. "Now, let's all get in this car and get the hell out of here."

"According to Faye, that's not much of a possibility," Kent said softly. He glared at the Alchemist, who stared at him in stunned amazement.

"MacIntyre?" he snarled. "You can't be here. The drug . . ."

"Didn't work so good," Kent completed. "Can't say that I'm all that sorry, either."

"You'll be sorry," Collingswood warned. "We'll all die without that helicopter."

Faye clutched at Kent's arm. "The helicopter wouldn't help. I told him he'd have a better chance of survival if he stayed on the ground. I told him if he used that much Mozelle in a pond this size—"

"She's lying!" Collingswood shouted. "She was trying to get me killed, too." He wrung his hands together. "I had to do it. I had to demonstrate . . . I had to show him that it worked. I had to. . . ." He blinked into Kent's face, and looked more terrified than ever. "Look, MacIntyre, I didn't mean to hurt her, I—"

"You'd better get in that trunk right now," Kent said very softly, very menacingly. "Otherwise, I will probably kill you with my bare hands."

"We'll die anyway," Collingswood growled. "Without that helicopter, we'll never get out of here in time."

"We'll see." Kent took one warning step toward him, and Collingswood hastily climbed into the trunk, beside the big blonde.

"What about the pilot?" Kent asked.

Dan slammed down the lid. "Unconscious in the back." He lifted an eyebrow at Kent. "Now what?"

"I'm thinking about it." Kent led Faye a few steps away from the car, and faced her, his arms resting on her shoulders while his amber-flecked eyes looked directly into hers. "You once said . . . uh . . . that the Wizard had the magic to defeat the Alchemist. Is that right?"

"Yes." She wiped her cheeks with her fingers, sniffing. "But now it's too late. Mozelle—"

"Not necessarily." He swallowed with some difficulty. "This . . . uh . . . Mozelle stuff—is there anything magnetic in it? Anything at all?"

"Magnetic?" Faye echoed. She wiped her wet cheeks with her fingers, and tried to find the answer to his question. "Some of the chemicals have magnetic properties, but . . ."

"And what would happen if the magnetic stuff was separated from the other stuff? Is that possible?"

"It's possible," she agreed blankly. "I don't know what it would do. We never tried . . ."

"Theoretically speaking, what would happen?"

She shook her head, unable to come up with a coherent thought. His gaze probed hers, calming her, clearing her panic. She took a breath and mentally ran through the complicated list of chemicals, trying to sort out the ones with the strongest magnetic properties. "The vaporization would still take place," she decided. "But I don't think the base reaction would work the same, and—" She opened her eyes, suddenly feeling alive with bright, glorious hope. "Without the copper sulfate, it wouldn't gather the toxins. It would just . . . go. . . . Oh, Kent, do you really think you can do that?"

His gaze intensified. "I don't know. Do you think I can?"

Faye searched his face for a long moment. "Of course," she answered, and she was absolutely, dead-certain positive. "I should have thought of it before. You're my Wizard. Of course, you can."

His entire body shuddered. "Oh, babe," he groaned. "I sure hope you're right." He turned to Dan, and quickly explained what he had in mind. "Faye says you have a better chance of survival if you stay on the ground. Will you take her and—"

"I'm not going!" Faye insisted. "I am staying here with you. An Ayaldwode stays with her Wizard, remember? Besides, it won't make any..."

Kent turned back to her. "Please," he begged. "Please. I can't concentrate when you're around."

"Kent..."

He captured her chin in his palm. "Listen to me, babe. I will not perform my trick unless you go with Dan. Please, just this once, do as I ask. Maybe I can slow it down, or maybe...something will happen. Let me believe I'm getting you out of this alive. Please?"

Faye read the determination in his face and regretfully nodded. "If that's what you want."

"It is." He held out his hand toward Dan. "Drive like hell, okay?" Dan took his hand, and Kent took an abrupt step forward, giving his counselor a brief man-to-man hug. "I'd better see you later," he said as he stepped out of the embrace.

"You'll see me, kid," Dan growled. "You've never let me down before and this is a hell of a time to start." They exchanged a long, meaningful look, then Kent turned to Faye and folded her into him. She felt his body trembling, felt the outpouring of his emotion, even though he was silent. He gave her a too-brief kiss and moved away.

"You are a Wizard, Kent," she assured him. "You can do this."

"We're about to find out." He turned, striding with long, determined steps toward the pond.

Faye turned to Dan. "Mr. Stuart, I—"

"We'll just go a little ways up the road to give the kid some space," Dan interrupted kindly. "I don't want to miss it, either."

THE CLOUDS IN THE SKY were reflected in the still, opaque water, their bright pink-and-orange glow an ominous warning that time was running out. He had maybe five minutes, Kent calculated. Five minutes before the top of the sun crept over the horizon. Five minutes before ultraviolet rays hit this pond. Five minutes before he, and two people very dear to him were destroyed—not to mention an entire town, and maybe a lot more. Lord, he wished he'd tried something like this before so he had some idea about the outcome.

He transmitted one last, fond thought to his sister, and felt her comforting support settle into his mind. She wasn't quite sure what was going on, but she had every confidence in his ability to survive. He kicked off his boots, almost grinning. He took a breath, then another, and turned his attention to the water.

He couldn't picture Mozelle, or the chemicals he was attempting to extract, but perhaps touching it would be just as useful. He took a tentative step into the murky pond, ignored the coldness of the water; and took another step, wading toward the center, pushing his hands down into it. Then he focused on the surface, on the rippling circles that signaled the presence of Mozelle.

The forest around him hushed to perfect stillness, as if every being there were holding a collective breath, waiting, hoping....

He pushed every other thought away, took a strong, mental photograph of the water in front of him, and the circles on top. Then he closed his eyelids and pictured those circles coming toward him, floating toward him, until he was surrounded by them, until the rest of the water was as clear and uninteresting as it must have been before.

"You are a Wizard," Faye had assured him. "You can do this."

He could feel the energy leaving him, the cold, clear tingling it left behind, and even the faint headache that accompanied it. Yet, when he opened his eyes, nothing seemed to be happening. The circles of water that signaled Mozelle remained.

Then, very, very faintly, almost as if he were imagining it, the pattern on the surface of the water began to change, forming a second figure, an almost skinlike parabola. It formed and reformed, and reformed again, swelling before him. The forest whispered a breath, the sun heaved itself over the horizon, Kent threw up his arms and a milky smog rose around him, an almost-living sphere. "Wow!" he muttered. He let out the breath he had been holding, and carefully arranged for the bubble to float away from him, over the weeds and grasses of the shore, and finally to the ground. He took a gasp of air, glanced up at the sky, and froze.

The sun was above the horizon now, its full spectrum striking the pond and reflecting brightly into his eyes. He'd be the first to know, Kent realized. If Faye had been wrong about Mozelle, if his little trick hadn't worked, he'd be the first victim of Mozelle. For Faye's sake, as well as his own, he hoped that wasn't what was going to happen. He remained there, his dark figure a shadow in the water, waiting for the verdict.

It was actually quite spectacular, and, under other circumstances, he might have been more appreciative of it. As the sun touched the water, each individual molecule seemed to ignite, moving upward, joining with others, forming a perfect mirror image of the pond, an image interrupted only by his presence. It hovered in the air and swayed gently with the slight breeze. One blink of an eye later, it was everywhere, blanketing the forest, the sky, all the world he could see, with a thick milky coating, leaving Kent standing in the murky pond, cold, wet, and very much alive.

Then it vanished. A car roared down the road. A lithe pixie figure leapt out of it and danced toward him, clapping her hands, while the forest around her chattered with relief. "I knew you could," she called as he waded back to shore. "I knew it! You see! You really *are* a Wizard, Kent! You really are!"

12

"THAT'S...VERY KIND of you," Faye murmured. She tried to swallow away the threatening tears as she blinked at the two short, rather plump gentlemen gathered around her.

One patted her shoulder consolingly. "I know it isn't going to be easy, Miss Merline, but it really is the best thing for you to do."

"I—I know," Faye stuttered. "I knew when I broke into the Sharade labs that it would come to this." She wiped her eyes with a finger, and glanced over her shoulder. There was quite a crowd gathered at the bottom of the path leading to her place. There were two or three officials from the government, the two WEA men, several people from Neverdale who'd come out to see what was going on, and Kent and Dan. Two of the officials were in the process of loading the Alchemist and his companions into cars.

"It does work," Collingswood was insisting. "I know it does. I don't know what happened. I..."

His blond henchman turned his back without speaking, led away by one of the officials. Collingswood went right on talking, repeating the same thing over and over. "It must work. It must."

Faye turned away. Things had happened as she'd anticipated—her Wizard had defeated the Alchemist, and now, it was time . . .

She spoke to her companions. "The break-in at Sharade. I did do it. Will there be . . ."

Both WEA men shook their heads. "Sharade has agreed to drop all charges," explained one. They glanced at their watches in perfect unison. "We can help you get a few of your things if you like."

Faye swallowed again. "No. No, that's . . . uh . . . not necessary." She gestured toward Kent. "Mr. MacIntyre . . ."

The men exchanged a look. "Of course."

Faye lifted her chin and wandered slowly toward Dan and Kent. They were leaning against Dan's car, watching the officials drive away. Kent was munching macadamia nuts and looking at her. He caught her eye, grinned, then slowly straightened as his smile faded with concern. Faye drew in a sigh. His jeans were wet and filthy, his brown shirt covered by an overlarge gray jacket. His darkly stubbled chin and bruised face added to his bedraggled appearance, but his eyes glittered with power and satisfaction. He was so tremendously attractive, her entire body quivered with longing. This was going to be very, very difficult.

He put a possessive arm around her. "Hey, babe. Those guys aren't giving you trouble, are they?"

"No," she whispered. "No, no. I . . . uh . . ." She circled his waist with her arm. "Would you come partway up to my place with me? My forest would like to thank you."

He eyed the trees warily. "It would, would it? That really isn't necessary, but I'll certainly come with you. You look about done in."

Faye swallowed again, and looked up at Dan. "Mr. Stuart, I don't know how to thank . . ."

He bowed his head gravely, his gray-eyed gaze meeting hers with wise knowing. "It was an honor," he said, and she knew he meant it.

"Thank you," Faye whispered. She stood on tiptoe to kiss his cheek, then took Kent's hand and led him into her forest.

Her forest did indeed want to thank him. The slight breeze pushed aside the canopy of leaves, allowing the sun to stream down and warm him. From around trees, from under bushes, from inside logs, the animals crept out to express their gratitude. A mother deer, her fawn tucked beside her, darted in front of them and stopped to stare. "It really wasn't that big a deal," Kent muttered as she led him along the path.

"It was so," Faye insisted. "It was their lives, Kent. You saved all this. They will never, ever forget. None of us will."

"That's . . . uh . . . swell," he grunted, but she could tell he was touched. He cleared his throat a couple of times. "Maybe next time I'm walking through this place, they will be kind enough to show me the way, instead of trying to get me lost."

Faye's heart gave a beat of warning. The moment had arrived. "I won't be here."

He gave her a puzzled look. "Where will you be?"

She stopped walking and faced him. "I don't know."

"What do you mean, you don't know?" His frown deepened. "Where are you . . ."

"I don't know, Kent." She took a shudder of a breath. "Those men from WEA . . . they are going to find me a place."

"Why?" He motioned up the hill. "You already have a place."

"Not anymore." She cupped her top teeth over her bottom lip and rubbed her hands together. "I can't stay here," she said softly. "Mozelle is a dangerous thing to know about."

"Yeah, but . . ." He thrust his fingers into his hair. "Collingswood is convinced that it's flawed. Besides, he's under arrest. They've got enough charges to hold him for a billion years."

Faye peered over his shoulder. Not far in front of them, a slight mist was beginning to form, a swirling, beckoning white cloud. "He knows I'm alive."

"So what?" Kent glanced down the hill. "That blond idiot works for his backer, and his backer will be very, very annoyed when he finds out his investment is not going to pay off. I wouldn't give Collingswood a whole lot of chances of remaining in one piece."

"I realize that." She put a hand on one of the arms he'd folded across his chest. "There will be others, Kent. Others who would do anything to get their hands on

Mozelle, and on the woman who knows its secret." She shook her head. "I don't want to go through this again. It is too dangerous for the world."

"Not to mention for you," he muttered. "Of course, you wouldn't worry about something like that, would you?"

She lifted her shoulders.

Kent took a breath. "So . . . uh . . . when are you going?"

Faye gestured behind him. "Now."

Kent swiveled his head to look over his shoulder. His shoulders tensed, and when he looked back at her, his dark eyes were wide with alarm. "Just a minute. What the hell is going on here?"

"I'm going away, Kent. I told you. When our mission is over, I . . ."

"Disappear," he completed. "But—" he shook his head "—no. This is ridiculous. You are *not* going to disappear. The WEA people are taking you someplace. Someplace . . . real."

"That's right," she admitted.

He stroked a shaking hand around his chin. "They can't arrange something like that on the spur of the moment. They'll take you to a safe house or a hotel or something. I can come—"

"You can *not* come with me, Kent."

"Sure, I can. I'll talk to them. They'll . . ."

She shook her head and pressed her lips together. "I don't want you to come."

His mouth dropped open, his hand coming up, a finger held out in schoolmarmish fashion. "That is *not* true, Faye." He took a step toward her, the heat from his body reaching hers. "You're in love with me. You said so. I heard you, and I was *not* dreaming!"

"That's right." A tear slid down her cheek. "I am in love with you, Kent. That's why I don't want you to come with me."

"This makes zero sense, babe." His arm came up to surround her, to try to pull her to him, but she resisted. "What's wrong?" he demanded. "I don't get it. *You* don't want it to be over. *I* don't want it to be over. Why...?"

She moved out of his embrace. "I'm an Ayaldwode. You are a Wizard."

"Of course. I should have known. Another one of these Wizard..."

"I don't like it, either!" Faye interjected. "And you are right. I don't want it to be over. But sooner or later, it will be over. You're a Wizard. You'll get restless."

"That doesn't just work one way," he argued. "You could..."

"No, I couldn't. When an Ayaldwode loves, it is forever. I know that is almost impossible for a Wizard. It isn't your fault. It is just part of a Wizard's nature." She wiped her eyes with a finger. "We both know what will happen. You will get restless and..." She trembled with a sigh. "I couldn't bear to see that happen. I couldn't."

Kent shifted his weight from foot to foot. "It might not," he muttered, but he didn't sound any more convinced than she was.

"It will," Faye said sadly. "That is why a Wizard and an Ayaldwode only have a short time together, and why the Ayaldwode must disappear. If she doesn't, she might fall in love with the Wizard, and that will only break her heart."

He stared at her for a long moment. Then his shoulders dropped into acceptance. "What about this? Isn't this parting breaking your heart? It sure isn't doing mine any good."

"I can live with this." She touched her tongue to her lips. "You don't want it to end—right now, anyway. And I can . . . I can take comfort in that."

He rubbed a palm over his face. "I don't feel all that comforted."

"It will pass," she assured him. "You'll stop feeling like this in a very little while." She smiled at him, loving him so much she ached with it. "You are a wonderful Wizard, Kent. Thank you so much for coming." She touched his cheek for one last time, feeling a tingling from the contact. "I'll never forget you. Ever."

She brushed her lips against his, then turned and walked away from him, into the drifting, floating, smoky fog, leaving her Wizard behind.

ONE MINUTE SHE WAS THERE, and the next, she was gone, swallowed by the dense mist, leaving him all alone in her forest. Kent stared after her for a long time, stunned by what had just happened. The inevitability of it settled around him like a shroud. He should have known it would come to this. Every single thing she'd said had come to pass. Their time together had been short, she was going to disappear...everything. He couldn't stop it from happening. If he hung around, he'd break her heart. He was lousy at commitment and terrible at "forever." Look what he'd done last time. He didn't want to do that to her.

He shoved his hands in his pockets and stumbled toward the road, nodding absently at the animals that came to watch. He hadn't expected it to turn out this way. He'd thought he'd have some time, make love to her on a real bed instead of in a cold, dark hut of some sort, listen to her stories, watch her, just . . . enjoy being with her.

He pushed aside a bush, and there it was—the place he'd seen her the first time he'd come up here. He sat down in the exact spot he'd sat then, and rested his back against the very same tree. Two brown-and-gray bunnies hopped out to stare at him with sympathetic eyes. They reminded him of her. Everything reminded him of her. He sat there, torturing himself with his memories, feeling worse and worse with each passing second. Avril intruded into his musings and he pushed her impatiently aside. He didn't need Avril right now; he needed Faye. Damn, but he was going to miss her. Already he missed her. Already he felt as if a wound had been opened that would never, ever heal. His chest constricted with a tight, terrible painfulness, and his head started to throb, warning that more pain was imminent. Damn!

A few minutes later, he heard the sound of heavy footfalls rustling through the underbrush, a bush waved slightly, and Dan pushed his way into view. "You okay, kid?" he asked.

Kent squinted up at him. "Been better." Lord, he'd never been worse. His heart was slamming so hard he couldn't breathe, and he could hardly speak around the horrible lump in his throat. He gestured toward the road. "She's . . . uh . . . going to be leaving with them."

"I know," Dan said gently.

Kent let his head fall back, grateful for the support of the tree. How long was he going to feel like this? If it was more than ten minutes, he wouldn't live through it.

Dan stood in front of him, hands shoved deep in his pants pockets, jiggling his change. "I sort of thought you two had something going."

"We did." Kent raised his hands and wiped his face, unsurprised to find it was damp. Man, he was in bad shape. "I'd only break her heart."

"Now why would you do something like that?"

"It wouldn't be intentional. It's just...my nature, and she . . ." He struggled to control his emotion. "She wouldn't be able to handle it."

"Probably not," Dan agreed. "So don't do it."

Kent clenched his back teeth. "Some things can't be changed, Dan. You know what I'm like."

"Thought I did. What do you think you're like?"

"Restless, easily bored, and difficult to understand," Kent answered promptly. Faye's words. Typical Wizard stuff. "Not good at commitment," he added.

Dan snorted. "Where did you get a damn fool idea like that? You've got a master's degree. That takes commitment."

"Not the right kind," Kent grumbled. Faye would be safe with those WEA people, he thought. He hoped they'd find her someplace nice, with her ferns and birds around to keep her happy. Would she find someone else—someone to share her life? He hated that idea; hated it a whole bunch.

"You've never let me down," Dan went on. "You've been a loyal brother to Avril." He lifted a shoulder. "Sounds like commitment to me."

"I was also married," Kent reminded him. "Look how that turned out."

"That was a mistake," Dan observed. "Didn't have much to do with commitment, though. You just didn't love her."

"I did love her," Kent insisted. No, he couldn't have. Wizards don't fall in love. "At least . . . I thought I did."

"Did you?" Dan scuffed his shoe in the dirt. "Why did you think that?"

"I . . . uh . . ." He couldn't talk about that now, not while his heart was shredding bit by bit. "I don't know," he muttered irritably. "Avril said—"

"I figured as much!" Dan interrupted, scowling. "Avril told you that you were in love, didn't she?"

Kent bent his head in silent agreement. That was pretty much how it had happened. Kent hadn't been positive, but Avril had been so insistent. "I didn't have to listen to her," he admitted.

"No, you didn't, and you shouldn't have! For pete's sake, Kent, that marriage doesn't prove anything! You didn't want to be married to the woman, you didn't love her, and you made no effort to make the marriage work. It was doomed from the start, not because you're incapable of keeping a commitment, but because you didn't make one!"

Kent stared at him. Dan was right. He hadn't made a commitment to that. He'd known it wouldn't work even while he was doing it. He had made other commitments, and he'd followed through on them. Perhaps he didn't have to share all the characteristics of a Wizard, just because he was one. After all, he was also a MacIntyre, and that certainly didn't mean he shared all of Avril's bad habits. For one thing, he didn't go around arranging her life for her.

Dan squinted down at him. "Do you love that little gal up there?"

Did he? He imagined her little person, standing in the Denver darkness, kneeling in the forest, sitting in her kitchen telling him stories, examining his body, desperately making love in a dark shed. He remembered how he'd felt when he thought she'd perish, and he thought about how he felt now. "Yes," he said slowly. "Yes, I love her." He watched his hands clench into fists. "But . . . it will pass."

No, that wasn't right. He was a Wizard. When a wizard falls in love, it's forever. Forever. Forever...

SHE CAME.

He'd been certain she would. However, when she finally stepped around a bush, an hour after she'd left him, Kent breathed a sigh of relief.

A slight fog accompanied her, winding around her as if to hold her back. She had changed into a pale brown dress, and she looked exactly as she had when they'd met at this spot before. Her face was drawn and sad, her steps heavy. She was carrying a large bag made of some brown material, and when she saw him, she stopped dead, squeezed her eyes shut and opened them.

"Hi, babe," he drawled.

She glanced around, then closed her eyes again. "K-Kent?"

"Uh-huh."

"What...uh..." Her tongue came out to touch her lips. "What are you doing here?"

"Me?" He pushed himself to his feet. "I'm waiting for an Ayaldwode. I understand one pops by here every so often."

"Kent, I—" she shook her head "—I wish you hadn't come," she whispered. "This is so hard for me. We—"

"I had to come," he interrupted. "Otherwise, we'd be having this little chat with an audience, and I'm nervous enough, as it is." He frowned at a squirrel who'd stopped to watch. "You don't need to be here, do you?"

The squirrel gave him a reproachful look and departed. Faye turned after it. "There's nothing left for us to say."

"Don't try to run off, babe," Kent warned softly. "I saved this forest, remember. It's on my side." To confirm that, a tree bent in a gust of wind, almost as if to block Faye's path.

She sighed and faced him. "Kent . . ."

He stared at her across the small space between them, his eyes looking directly into hers. The haze appeared to thicken, and Kent realized his heart rate was up in the danger zone. He was nervous, all right. Hell, he was scared half to death. He breathed deeply, and tried to control the tremor in his voice. "I love you. I want you to marry me."

Faye dropped her bag, and her silver-blue eyes got even larger in her already pale face. "I can't. I told you. You'd . . ."

Kent took a quick step forward and wrapped his fingers around her arms. "You told me a whole bunch of stuff I should have ignored."

"You can't ignore it," she argued. "You're a Wizard. You can't stop being one."

"I'll take pills," Kent muttered. He took a breath. "Look, I might be a Wizard, but that doesn't mean I have all of their genetic characteristics. I love you, Faye. I am quite capable of making a commitment to you and keeping it."

"Oh, Kent." She stroked his cheeks with both her hands. "I know you mean that now, but a Wizard gets restless . . ."

"Do you have any other reason, besides this Wizard stuff, to think I'll do that?"

She blinked. "No, but . . ."

"Then, if you really loved me, you'd give me a chance to prove that I can be different."

"I do love you." Her eyes filled with tears. "I love you and I always will. But a Wizard—"

"No Wizard insults Faye!" Kent insisted. "I know my track record isn't the greatest, but this is *not* the same. I am not going to get restless and break your heart. I wouldn't do that to someone I love, and I love you. That is not going to change. Not ever."

Faye's eyes widened. Her mouth opened slightly, her little pink tongue came out to moisten her lips. "How long?" she whispered. Her face flooded with color, her eyes were glowing bright gleams of hope. "How long did you say you'd love me?"

Kent gazed into her darling, upturned face. "I will love you forever," he promised, and he knew, without a doubt, that this time, he meant it.

"YOU MEAN YOU WOULD HAVE left if I hadn't said 'forever'?" Kent demanded incredulously.

Faye sat on the floor of her forest, snuggled up to her Wizard. The haze surrounding her was gone, leaving her absolutely euphoric with delight at what had just happened. She was still going to have to leave this place, but she was going to be with him for forever and it was almost too wonderful to be believed. "I didn't know you felt that way," she murmured. "I know when a Wizard falls in love, it's forever, but I didn't know…"

Kent raised her chin with a finger and gave her a look that tried to be stern, but was too filled with happiness and relief to accomplish it. "There'd better not be any more little gems I'm supposed to say. Or, if there are, they'd better come with cue cards!"

"There aren't." She touched his dear, dear face. "Oh, Kent, I love you ever so much."

"I love you, too, babe. I swear you won't regret this. I swear." His lips met hers, and she responded with total enthusiasm. Of course, she wouldn't regret it.

Something in his pocket made a crackling noise. "Oh, yeah," Kent mumbled. "I almost forgot." He tugged a two-way radio out of his back pocket, fiddled with a dial and spoke into it. "Pan to Hook. Pan to Hook. Tinker Bell is in the bag. Over."

There was dead silence, then Dan's growl: "I gather she said yes."

"You bet!" Kent grinned triumphantly and tossed the radio onto the ground. "Now, where were we?"

"We were, uh—"

"I remember," he interrupted. He folded her to him again and began nuzzling into her shoulder.

"Kent," Faye murmured. "Why…uh… Why was Dan…uh…"

"Hmm?" He brushed his lips around her neck, heading toward her mouth. "Oh, he's just getting it all organized."

"Getting what organized?" she breathed.

"Our wedding." He touched the tip of his tongue to her ear. "There won't be time for much of a ceremony now, but all of Neverdale are doing their best to make it special."

Faye tilted her head and arched toward him. "Why would they do that?" she asked, with a hazy, happy sigh. "We just got married. We don't need to do it again."

Kent's head came up in a jerk. "I guess I'd better get used to it," he muttered. "My entire life is going to be like this." He paused, his lips moving into a wide, satisfied smile. "And I'm going to enjoy every second. Okay. Go ahead. Lay it on me. How did we manage to have a wedding that I don't remember?"

"You do remember," Faye insisted. "It just happened." She decided it was her turn to taste his earlobe, and found it was incredibly intoxicating. "We were here in the forest and we promised to love each other forever. That's how Ayaldwodes get married."

"Ah." He brushed his mouth over hers, and sighed. "That's terrific, but unfortunately not recognized in other parts of the globe, like, say, ten feet from here. We have to do it all over again, but this time, a whole town will be staring at us, and someone will tell me what I'm supposed to say."

Faye undid a button on his shirt and slipped her hand inside. "If that's what you want to do, I don't mind. When would you like—"

"Now," he interrupted. She glanced around, and he quickly went on. "Not right now, darling. We have to leave here, drive to Neverdale, and *then* get married. You, of course, look absolutely adorable, and I, unfortunately, look and smell like a swamp creature, but we'll just have to keep our wedding pictures well hidden."

Faye studied him critically. "You look wonderful," she decided. "Fabulous. Very Wizardly. But maybe I should talk to the WEA. . . ."

"They're okay with this. As a matter of fact, they're quite delighted." He sucked her earlobe. "It accomplishes everything they wanted to accomplish. You get a new name, a new country, and a new place to live. I'll be there to protect you, and, as long as you're around to fix my magnetic field every now and then, you should be perfectly safe. We'll get a place outside Calgary and we'll stock it with birds and ferns and whatever else an Ayaldwode needs to keep her happy."

It sounded like a dream come true. Then Faye had another thought. "What about your sister? How does she feel about this?"

"She's livid." Kent sounded pleased at the prospect. "Actually, she's torn between absolute fury, total shock, and almost pathological curiosity." He lifted his head and frowned at her. "How about your relatives? They aren't going to turn me into a frog if they don't like the idea, are they?"

"Absolutely not," Faye said firmly. "It's impossible to do that when you're this far north of the equator."

Kent let out a hoot of laughter, and kissed her soundly. "Are our children going to be Ayaldwodes or Wizards?"

"We'll have one of each," Faye decided, entranced by the idea. "Or maybe two of each."

"Uh-huh. What are little Ayaldwodes like?"

"Good-natured, kind and very sweet."

"Uh-huh. And little Wizlings?"

"Mischievous, disobedient, naughty..."

"I'd like to see for myself." He kissed her again. "And since we've already had an Ayaldwodian-style marriage, I believe we can get started on that right away." He slid his hand up her dress and began lowering them to the ground.

"Kent!" Dan's voice hollered over the two-way radio. "You're supposed to be proposing, not consummating! Get down here!"

Kent sighed, straightened Faye's clothes and got reluctantly to his feet. As he rose, an unexpected gust of wind swirled around him, rustling the leaves, caressing through his hair. He froze, his eyes focusing into the distance, as if he was hearing a voice. Then the leaves settled back to earth, forming a strange, circular pattern in the dust at his feet.

Faye stood beside him and squeezed his hand. Apparently her relatives approved, after all.

Temptation

brings you...

Bestselling Temptation author Elise Title is back with a funny, sexy, three-part mini-series. **The Hart Girls** follows the ups and downs of three feisty, independent sisters who work at a TV station in Pittsville, New York.

In **Dangerous at Heart (Temptation August '95)**, a dumbfounded Rachel Hart can't believe she's a suspect in her ex-fiancé's death. She only dumped Nelson—she didn't bump him off! Sexy, hard-edged cop Delaney Parker must uncover the truth—or bring Rachel in.

Look out for Julie Hart's story in **Heartstruck (Temptation September '95)**. Kate Hart's tale, **Heart to Heart**, completes this wonderful trilogy in October '95.

MILLS & BOON

are proud to present...

A set of warm, involving romances in which you can meet
some fascinating members of our heroes' and heroines'
families. Published each month in the Romance series.

Look out for "A Bittersweet Promise" by Grace Green
in October 1995.

Family Ties: Romances that take the family to heart.

This month's
irresistible novels from

Temptation

HEARTSTRUCK by Elise Title

Second in *The Hart Girls* trilogy

Julie Hart had reluctantly agreed to co-host a TV talk show
with heart-throb Ben Sandler. The ratings soared as she
challenged the guests and even ended up hitting the charming
Ben! But there was no denying the chemistry between them,
both on *and off* the set.

MAD ABOUT YOU by Alyssa Dean

Faye—an innocent, lost in the big city—had charmed Kent
MacIntyre, until she had stolen his files. He found her hiding
place only to learn that she desperately needed his help. A
world-weary, cynical investigator, Kent knew damn well not to
trust any woman. Why did he so want to believe her?

UNDERCOVER BABY by Gina Wilkins

Detective Dallas Sanders had taken part in some unusual
undercover operations, but cracking the baby-smuggling ring
was the toughest. Especially since it meant playing the part of
an unwed, pregnant woman. Even worse, she had to pretend to
be head over heels in love with no-good Sam Perry.

PLAYBOY McCOY by Glenda Sanders

Laurel Randolph had all the "facts" on McCoy. But she pushed
aside any nagging doubts when she embarked on a shipboard
fling with him. Under the hot tropical sun, McCoy made her
feel sexy...desirable...loved. But was it the real thing?

Spoil yourself next month
with these four novels from

HEART TO HEART by Elise Title

Third in *The Hart Girls* trilogy

Kate Hart had had too many run-ins with Mr. Wrong and she
would be darned if she would let Brody Baker smooth-talk his
way into her heart…and into her bed. No matter *how* sexy he
was!

THE TROUBLE WITH BABIES by Madeline Harper

Cal Markam was Annie Valentine's toughest case. She was
hired to mould the millionaire playboy into a conservative
company president, but a rumour was circulating that he had
fathered twins! A man like Cal could only mean trouble.
Double trouble.

SERVICE WITH A SMILE by Carolyn Andrews

Sunny Caldwell was determined to succeed and had two
golden rules—to put her personal delivery service first and
never to get involved with a client. She followed her rules until
the day she met Chase Monroe and his needy family.

PLAIN JANE'S MAN by Kristine Rolofson

Plain Jane won a man. Well, not exactly. Feisty and
independent Jane Plainfield won a boat. The man, gorgeous
boat designer Peter Johnson, just seemed to come with it!

GET 4 BOOKS
AND A MYSTERY GIFT

Return this coupon and we'll send you 4 Temptations and a mystery gift absolutely FREE! We'll even pay the postage and packing for you.

We're making you this offer to introduce you to the benefits of Reader Service: FREE home delivery of brand-new Temptations, at least a month before they are available in the shops, FREE gifts and a monthly Newsletter packed with information.

Accepting these FREE books and gift places you under no obligation to buy, you may cancel at any time, even after receiving just your free shipment. Simply complete the coupon below and send it to:

MILLS & BOON READER SERVICE, FREEPOST, CROYDON, SURREY, CR9 3WZ.

No stamp needed

Yes, please send me 4 free Temptations and a mystery gift. I understand that unless you hear from me, I will receive 4 superb new titles every month for just £1.99* each postage and packing free. I am under no obligation to purchase any books and I may cancel or suspend my subscription at any time, but the free books and gifts will be mine to keep in any case. (I am over 18 years of age)

2EP5T

Ms/Mrs/Miss/Mr _____

Address _____

_____

_____ Postcode _____